Change Me

Andrej Blatnik

Change Me

Translated by Tamara M. Soban

DALKEY ARCHIVE PRESS

McLean / Dublin

Library of Congress Cataloging-in-Publication Data

Names: Blatnik, Andrej, author. | Soban, Tamara,
translator.
Title: Change me / Andrej Blatnik ; translated by
Tamara M. Soban.
Other titles: Spremeni me. English
Description: First edition. | McLean : Dalkey Archive
Press, 2019. | Summary: "Andrej Blatnik's ambitious
novel tells the story of a man's determination to
redically change himself and to alter the world that
has embraced globalization as the God of the
future"-- Provided by publisher.
Identifiers: LCCN 2019030343 | ISBN
9781628973365 (paperback)
Classification: LCC PG1919.12.L38 S6713 2019 |
DDC 891.8/435--dc23
LC record available at https://
lccn.loc.gov/2019030343

Dalkey Archive Press
McLean, IL / Dublin

www.dalkeyarchive.com

Printed on permanent/durable acid-free paper.

This one is for you. You know?

Nothing is coincidental or unintentional.

One day he prayed to the God of Israel, "Please bless me and give me a lot of land. Be with me so I will be safe from harm." And God did just what Jabez had asked.

1 Chronicles 4,10

I was looking back to see if
You were looking back at me
To see me looking back at you.

Massive Attack, *Safe from Harm*

How can I stay the same
How can I protect
Myself from change
Only through change

EKV, Modro i zeleno (Indigo and Green)

Thanks to

Bernardo A. for jail stories.

Blade Runner for the sense of being a slave.

Heinrich B. for the guitar player with a hat.

Jorge Luis B. for knife fighting.

Igor B. for the cup of coffee.

Ian C. for finding one's destiny.

Ivan C. for the flames that change.

Clarissa Pinkola E. for the cells screaming.

Wilhelm G. for what love teaches you.

Michel H. for the striptease.

Irena J. for the field report.

Don de L. for the tour of the supermarket.

Curzio M. for the disgrace of victory.

Haruki M. for the call from afar.

Kakuzo O. for the future that is behind us.

Michael O. for renouncing society.

Orban P. for onscreen kisses.

Zoran P. for the influxes from the East.

Manuel R. for the Angel of Vengeance and fatherly advice.

Wislawa S. for a piece of true love.

Džoni Š. for the phantom of freedom.

Bonnie T. for the good men gone.

Olga T. for pausing to think before sinking in the teeth.

Paulinho da V. for those verses.

And to all who read fragments and those who read it all.

1.

Let's do it now, let's end this story, you and me, we've waited long enough. You told me to tell you when it's over—it's over now. Everything happens eventually.

Remember the time we flipped through that book with too many colors? Somebody had flown around the world with a camera and viewed everything from the air. You asked me how come I never took pictures, traveling around as much as I did. I like to remember things through my own eyes, I told you. Through my eyes is the right way; my eyes see everything, except me. That's the way I want to remember the world, I told you, as if I hadn't been there. I don't want to be there, I told you, and I said it over and over, and you said I looked just like I was crying.

Well. I didn't want to look like I was crying. Anyway, I didn't want to talk about this. I wanted to say something else: It's here now, this story, all of it. It's here to say: I love you. I know, you're embarrassed, you're thinking this isn't the thing to say, it's too easy. Don't think that. It's not easy.

And don't be embarrassed. It's something you need to know. How many more times in life are you going to hear the words: I love you? They're very important words. You should listen to them.

This story is over. There will be others. There's room in them for you too. And for me. There's plenty of room.

I'm all right. I hope you are too.

2.
Whole-Beat Waltz

SOMETIMES, THINGS MUST change. And they do.

It all changed in an instant. When Monika came home from work around seven, as usual, Borut wasn't there. The boys were each in front of his own screen, as was usual when Borut wasn't there. Monika first turned off a fight between robots and mutants, then prancing elves in miniskirts. Ignoring the boys' shouts of protest, she picked up the containers with stale fries off the floor and asked where Daddy was.

The boys replied they were hungry. Feeling tired, as usual, Monika poured some healthy cereal into bowls to tide them over, then, realizing there wasn't enough food in the house because Borut had obviously failed to stock up, called for a pizza delivery. As soon as they heard her placing the order the boys pushed away their bowls of cereal. Milk splashed onto the tabletop and Monika tried to wipe it off with the sleeve of her sweaty blouse. There was a bunch of flowers in a vase in the center of the table as usual, but the newspaper was folded up on one of the chairs. Borut always read with such passion that the paper ended up crumpled and stained with sweaty thumb-marks and food smudges, so that Monika felt too disgusted to touch it. This time he'd obviously not even opened it. She asked again where Daddy was.

The boys were leafing through their heroic comics and, when she insisted, muttered irritably that he'd just downloaded the latest episode of *Space Terminators* on their play machine a little while ago. But they didn't go play then because they were watching cars crashing on television. And when they tried to play later, the play machine had already auto-locked. They glared at Monika, then the elder one asked in a saccharin, teary voice if Borut had really not told her the latest log-in code.

The code was probably in the file in which Borut kept a record of all his complicated chains of financial investments, life insurance policies, and purchases of replacement tissue for all four of them, but the last thing Monika wanted at the moment was an encounter with *Space Terminators*. She wanted a hot bath with essential oils and a glass of wine from the bottle Borut had said cost so much money an Indian family could live off it for six months. But it wasn't time yet. The world needed to be put in order, milk was trickling off the table and dripping onto the floor. Taking the vase with the flowers into the bedroom as usual and wiping the table, she realized there was no getting around it—she would have to bend down and proceed below, whither the thin milky trail led.

There were more scattered fries and crumpled fast-food packages under the table. The boxes were an unmistakable sign—something was wrong. Very wrong. Having given up on her, Borut indefatigably persisted in trying to feed the boys foods like bean sprouts, dried fruit, legumes, and nuts. Ordering fast food to saturate the boys with trans fats must have entailed a terrible struggle with his conscience. He'd always hand the money to the student making the delivery with his arm stretched out as far as it would go, as though he was afraid of catching the junk food bug by touching him; afterwards, he'd rush into his room, leaving them alone at the table.

One time, Monika got fed up with his sweaty brow and pursed lips as he clutched the delivery menu and paced about the apartment, looking for a solution that couldn't be found, while the boys kept popping out of their room every few minutes, "Is the pizza here yet? Is the pizza here yet?" and Borut heaving a sigh every time. "The kids like it, Borut," she said.

He gave her a look that made her regret having spoken; it occurred to her that she really should take matters into her own hands in moments of such clamoring for food, and leave Borut in peace to bend over his machines, withdrawn from reality, his favorite state. The boys' tastes followed the dictates of the world, no matter how hard Borut tried to bend them in another direction. When he told the boys there would be no more fast food, they managed on their own. They entered every stuff-your-face contest they could find, just to get their hands on their favorite morsels. Try as hard as they could, they never even made it to the second level, never mind won; other kids always devoured much more, being more used to the well-known brands of food the sponsors provided, while the two of them got sick too quickly since Borut wouldn't take them to training sessions at restaurant chains, and Monika didn't have the time to, as her job involved working with people and demanded all of her.

The boys didn't find losing as tragic as she'd expected they would. During the competition they could eat as much genetically modified stuff as they wanted and anyway the prizes were packages of food for people in need, and nobody wanted to eat those, not even people in need, least of all the winners of the competitions, so they tended to be left behind under the tables. Most of the winners were quite happy with having their victorious smiles pasted on the billboards of the fast food sponsors until the next competition—and with the calories they'd consumed.

Borut didn't dare stop the boys from entering such occasions of collective gorging; he felt that if rumors of his curbing their competitiveness reached the ears of the school counselors, they would send an intervention team to their house and have the boys transferred to some sort of better socialized care. Monika sometimes thought that she should tell him the system wasn't that expeditious, but then, if he knew how complex the procedure for child removal due to social neglect was, usually taking so long that the child grew up in the meantime, he would have asserted his will more. He'd refuse to take the boys to competitions and then *she* would have to do it, because otherwise the boys would suffer and Monika didn't want the boys to suffer. *If anyone has to suffer, it'd better be Borut,* she thought. *It's his fault anyway. There's no need to swim against the current.*

She went into Borut's room. Everything was neat and tidy, which was not unusual for Borut, and his machines were shut down, which was unthinkable. Borut's circuit boards usually purred all night long; if he wasn't doing business or listening to music, he was exchanging files with faceless and nameless friends he knew nothing about, not even whether they lived on another continent or in the apartment next door. They communicated in a jargon that the uninitiated such as Monika could not fathom, and came up with forever new ways of coding the sounds they were mashing up on their machines and sending to one another to digest and evaluate. She didn't know what he did, except for what he told her the first time she'd asked: putting together the *ultimate mix*. When she asked to hear some of his music, he first gazed at her for a long time, then softly said that he wasn't quite done yet, that the music wasn't *persuasive* enough yet. Then he bent over his machines again. Monika wanted to continue the conversation, she wanted to understand what the sense of the hours spent in his room was, and she said *but it's interesting you should be doing this when you never studied music*. Borut pondered her words. Then he told her that one was more easily persuasive without really intending it, and Monika thought again that life was perhaps too short for her to know Borut quite that well and wondered again whether that meant that things were not what they should be between them. *The secret of success: Getting to the bottom of every human resource.* She had no reason not to believe she always successfully did so at work, and she could not reasonably hope that she always successfully did so at home.

There was nothing for her in Borut's room, so she went into her room to see if he'd sent her a message. And he had; amidst the avalanche of spam and work-related email that started pouring into her personal account the minute she walked out of her office there flashed the name of the sender: *Me*.

The subject line read *Into You* (which between them meant *for your eyes only*) and the message was encrypted with their usual key for minor intimacies, the code that, unlike all the others, Monika could type in from memory, without having to refer to her codebook.

Dear M,

I'm gone, as you can see. Let's say it's only temporary. That it'll change. But there's just no other way at the moment. Thanks for understanding. I stuck it out as long as I could. You know, for a long time, I believed the family was the thing. That we had to be there for one another. That that was enough. That other things didn't matter. But they do. I know that now.

You probably think everything changed in a moment. It didn't. It happened very slowly. I spent a long time watching the boys sleep at night. I'd stand by the door, listening to them breathe. Their breathing was peaceful. They didn't sense what I was contemplating. They didn't know I had a secret bank account with enough money stashed away to last me two years. The key to another apartment in my pocket. I'd do that night after night. And every night I learned the same thing. The thing I also knew by day. That they shouldn't find out what they didn't know. Happiness built on a lie. Is that right? I was waiting for them to leave. So that I wouldn't have to. Is that right? The fear you feel above an abyss. Not the fear that you might lose your footing and fall. That's what children are afraid of. But the fear that it's only up to you. To stay or to jump. And the fear because you're considering both options.

I'm gone now. You think that's terrible. But it isn't. You're wrong. There's more than enough money for the three of you. You know that anyway. That won't be a problem. And the boys will be pleased that you'll be spending more time with them. They miss you. I'll be with them too. Again. Just not for a while. They have a stockpile of me. They know that. There are other things I have to do. I know that. Now.

Perhaps we'll see each other soon. Somewhere else, different. Don't go looking for the other woman. There isn't one. That would've been too easy. There are other things.

I'll be all right. I hope you'll be too.
B.

Monika reread the message. And again. Both times she stopped at the bit about the abyss. And thought—before the rush of cold anger at things having gotten out of hand and being dumped, before scratching the liquid crystal display with the diamond in her wedding ring—that Borut hadn't written something this long in quite a while.

She had felt him changing for a long time. His eyes. The way he held his glass. The way he sat at the table and bent his head before taking the first bite. The way he no longer raised his voice at the boys but merely repeated his words once and then backed off. He was changing. But she still saw the man with whom she'd seen thousands of kisses on their travels, or sitting in cafés, or watching movies, or shows, or concerts. Thousands of declarations of elected proximity. And had perhaps also exchanged just as many. The man with whom she'd been together thousands of times when the sound of the world was dying. The man with whom she still shared the same bed most nights couldn't be all that different from the man she'd chosen when she felt it was time to choose. Not that different. But she'd felt him changing.

She'd expected a change for a long time. She'd become accustomed to his going away; as long as he didn't go away after sleeping with her—that would've been humiliating. Having a room to herself wasn't bad. She always brought home so much work from the office it was crowded if Borut was there as well. But his going away meant something was not the way it had been, that something was wrong. And when she lay alone in their bed thinking about what was going on inside the man in the room next door, she was getting ready. What would she do if Borut was no longer with her some day? If the pledge was broken? How would she deal with such betrayal? What does one do in such cases? Of course it happens, it happens to others too, but people don't talk much about things like that, not even to friends, and Monika no longer had any friends, her job had taken its toll. She didn't know what a person did. But she did know this: When it came to it, it would be horrible, there would be pain. She hoped she was only afraid of it the way she was senselessly afraid of absurd things: Of cutting herself while slicing bread for the boys and being in pain. Of spraining her ankle going down the stairs too fast and being in pain. Of having some insane driver come careening down the highway on her side and crashing into her, and of being in pain and dying. She knew all those things were highly unlikely, although there *were* people who cut themselves with a knife. Who sprained their ankles. Who were crashed into by insane drivers driving on the wrong side of the highway. But she could nonetheless hope to be spared those pains.

Now she knew. It hadn't changed in a moment, not at this moment, but it was at this moment that she knew it had changed. And that now it would have to start all over. Differently. But first, the past would have to be erased. The relationship was over, the pledge broken. *Don't let him come back.* If he's left her once, he could leave her again, anytime. You can't count on a person like that. In business, one can afford to be defeated, one can lose— *sometimes*. It's part of the game. One has to lose so that the other can win, that's what it's all about, there's no other way. But not when it comes to love and family, which in time become one and the same thing. There, things have to be rock-solid and unshakable. And now everything had shifted. Things would have to be different. Different.

The doorbell rang. She took the pizza, and giving a big tip, eyed the well-built young man who delivered it, wondering whether she should tell him to come back later when the boys were in bed so he could deliver something else. She refrained from speaking, noticing he'd caught her sizing him up and stood waiting with the money in his hand to see what would come next. He took a couple of steps backwards, swaying his hips suggestively and hanging back. She felt like demanding her change back, recanting her generous "It's all right." She'd be within her rights to do so. Nothing was all right. But all she did was close the door and listen to his footsteps clattering down the stairs.

The boys wolfed down the pizza before she'd taken her shower, dried her hair, and did her makeup again. She coldly turned down their demands for further helpings of fries, robots, and mutants. The boys were taken aback; they were only used to such treatment from their father. Mommy always gave them anything they wanted, as much of it as they wanted, Mommy loved them unconditionally. They got into their pajamas with prints of superheroes without a fuss, just looking at each other dumbfounded. Something had changed—something had very obviously changed. Daddy had left before Mommy came home on many occasions, but he had never ordered fries for them before leaving, and Mommy had never forbidden fries when she came home. Life would obviously be different. Before getting into their beds they hugged tightly instead of having their usual evening scuffle, as though realizing they only had tonight left as children, that already in the morning they might have to grow up.

Monika declared goodnight and went to check on the balances in the family accounts. Borut was right. Those two years he had put money aside for didn't even show. There was more than enough money. With dismay she realized that she felt like this for the first time in her life. Something had changed. *She* had changed. She checked in the mirror but couldn't see anything noticeable. She was a few minutes older than before taking her shower, the lines in her face had undoubtedly deepened, but suddenly this had ceased to matter. She felt that with this concern dissipating, the real pain was coming. The pain she'd been afraid of. The pain she'd been expecting.

She went to the boys' room to take another look at them. They were asleep. Their breathing was peaceful even though she'd locked all the play machines. They were asleep all right, no doubt about it. She set up the baby alarm and put on her shoes. Not by car, she told herself. Not far. The boys might wake up screaming in terror in the middle of the night for the first time in their lives. She must stay close by. Stay close, but still go. Something had changed. Everything would have to be reorganized. It wasn't too late.

3.
Chipped Polka

Something had changed. Everything would have to be reorganized. It wasn't too late. Nighttime is the right time to realize that, thought Borut. The best things happen at night, in the car. A car is a place of untamed, unlimited freedom, you're unplugged from the world. The road changes into living tissue, into a body that responds to your touch, moving, stretching, receding from sight and contact. You can chase it without ever having to catch it. Because there's always another body after this one, and another road after this one, and another; you can never travel them all.

During his all-night drives Borut learned the language of roadside restaurants, junctions, signposts, side roads. He learned the beauty of the outlines of woods, the dark patches of waters, and the slants of hills. He learned to ignore the beauty of lit-up billboards. His country, which had always seemed too small, became endless as he explored its secret bends. Its roads were long and empty. Hardly ever did a car swish by. How very odd that there should be other people, he thought at such moments.

The best things happen at night; *did the devil make the world while God was sleeping,* rasped the voice in Borut's loudspeakers. Borut was never lonely in his car, he had music to keep him company, gigabytes of music he had stockpiled in his previous life without ever having the time to listen to it. Whenever sleep began to creep in on him he'd turn on the subwoofer and have the percussion pulsate the air with its regular beat. When he felt the landscape melting away too fast, he'd let flutes made of apricot wood fill the air, and the world would put on the brakes again. His choice made things different.

During the all-night drives there was plenty of time to think. Borut was letting his old self seep out of the car; the new man taking shape behind the wheel was different, calmer, more independent, there was something about gripping the leather-covered steering wheel that one could rely on, something about the neon blurs slipping along the windshield as the vehicle sped past advertising signs. *Pronouncements of various branches of the same global greed. Past. Nothing sticks anymore.*

There was no longer any feverish tallying up of the world, no more translating every mile covered into the number of bugs splattered against the windshield, the amount of pollutants emitted into the air, the additional nuclear troops deployed close to some drying oil wells. When such depressive math returned anyway, he would repeat to himself over and over: It doesn't matter. *It doesn't matter.* The mantra was senseless, *it did matter*, he knew it did, but this matter would have to wait for him to come back to it later. Now other things mattered more, closer things, things that were more *his*.

Borut was no newcomer to all-night drives. He had experienced them years before. It was different back then, though. He hadn't been the driver, but a passenger. Their bachelor's theses awaiting their respective professors' perusal, he and the girl that was later to become his wife—there was no other way— had journeyed all over the East. Thousands upon thousands of miles. The world was still a big place, and traveling a test. Buses drove along never-ending roads. One amorphous town followed another. People would get on and off, the two of them spoke to some, others spoke among themselves. But mostly they kept silent. And traveled. The confraternity of the lonely manifested in the slight incline of the head indicating where a toilet could be found at some rundown bus stop. The loudspeakers boomed during the rides, but people slept, their heads lolling as the driver steered the vehicle, landing from time to time on the shoulders or in the laps of unknown fellow passengers. A little discomfort, an apology, and again escape into sleep. On screens, films in numerous unknown languages succeeded one another, people killing and kissing, fighting and embracing. By the end of the journey they'd seen thousands of flickering kisses. During every one of them silence would mantle the passengers. During every one of them, people drifted into their own memories, their own pains. Every now and then a serene smile would play on someone's lips. "Are you going home?" Borut was wont to ask then. People would give him an astonished look, not understanding what the young foreigner wanted from them, and Borut stopped asking. Traveling in silence was not a bad way to travel. It gave him time to think about his own kisses, with the girl that would become his wife sitting by his side; sometimes she leaned her head against his shoulder, reached for his hand, and fell asleep. It seemed their journey would last forever.

The best things happen at night, and the best part of it was that night meant leaving the frenzy of the day behind. Though the world constantly strove to be higher, faster, stronger, most of it slept at night, which gave those awake time to meet their own selves. The journey to oneself is long even if you only travel it in your mind, thought Borut. He knew how pointless it was to think about what had been, but he thought about it anyway. It was hard to think of anything else. Of course, there were the boys. But the children were there all the time; from the moment they had first cried he thought of them nonstop; they had become a vital part of him as much as his own heart pumping blood or his lungs drawing breath. This couldn't possibly change as long as he lived. He breathed, his blood flowed, and he had children. But some other things were different. Could be different. That was the difference that needed to be made.

He pulled up outside the collection center. Lifting two boxes out of the trunk, he placed them on a trolley. A few dozen pounds. Too much for him. Too little for them. He gave the guard the usual batch of insider information that opened doors to places not everyone could enter, nothing classified, almost public knowledge, which was nonetheless beyond most investors, and put a finger to his lips, as usual, and, as usual, the guard nodded and, stepping back, began rifling through the papers and rummaging in his pocket for his cell phone at the same time. *His stockbroker doesn't get many a good night's sleep. Always these instructions in the middle of the night.* There was no other way; if he wanted to make a profit, the guard had to get on this in the dark. And if Borut wanted to see, he had to come in the dark. When he noticed after his first few times there that the management had clearly cleaned everything up before his announced visits and that the children stared at him unflinchingly when he walked through the door, he started coming on the sly. The view from behind the doorway saw more and was clearer.

The arrangement in the center had not changed since his last visit. Obviously, the sponsors were happy with the current state of affairs. Each simple barrack was done up according to the image of a different trademark. The inhabitants did not care about the color of the walls as long as they got something for free—or so they thought. Thus the Muslims did not know that the red of their hut was not the color of the crescent, but rather the color of a pig-processing company that was trying to get into the southern markets with the slogan *Eat pork!* It was slow going, but it worked.

From behind the doorway, Borut peered into the room of a Muslim family. It was different than the last time. It was different every time he came. The amount of television in the air was growing. Forever more and new children would sit on the couch for hours on end, watching the glorious world of home shopping. And as Allah bears no gifts, as Buddha is not a giver, they asked Santa for slimming belts. Their mothers caressed their potbellies. No relief packages had found their way to their door in a long time.

The next hut housed African Serbians. When bombs began falling on their capital, they fled the country, fled the continent, fled south, and settled in the country of a kinder dictator. He sold them citizenship and let them buy up the estates sold by the early white settlers, now hastening back to their primal homeland where they knew no one and no one knew them. But the proceeds from these sales turned out to be insufficient to fatten the dictator's offshore accounts, maintain his complex machinery of control, and feed the growing famine at the same time, so he decided to sell the country all over again, this time to its natives. He graciously allowed the African Serbians to purchase exit visas and the national airline took its final flights, some planes not returning from foreign airports; creditors were trying to recover their debts and the crews went in search of a better future. Some African Serbians had made it here, to these cream-painted huts sponsored by a confectionery company, in the hope that someone here would know them, that someone among those many who had gone north to find work would recognize them as relatives. But they were too numerous, and the ties too few. So they stayed here, did whatever work they could find, handed over the arranged percentage to the management, traded the rest for their daily bread, and waited for the next war.

The first time he set foot in the collection center, a whole new world opened before Borut's eyes. Of course he'd known that some people lived differently than him, he even knew some of them personally and exchanged a few words with them from time to time. But when the Chairman told him to visit the center and just look, to get some new ideas for the new markets, Borut had no clue that this was another one of the clever, simple little things the Chairman did to motivate the world to shift its position, and particularly his own business indicators. All it took was having a coffee with these displaced persons and Borut realized there were worlds that his profound taglines did not speak to. Worlds that did not hear his advertising messages or, in case they did hear them, failed to understand them and therefore couldn't buy what Borut's ads were selling. Of course everyone in the business knew that there were other worlds, but they were well hidden behind the first one, and everyone hoped it would remain that way. Of course, images would emerge from these other worlds. Of course he saw people sleeping in the street also in his own city—people who had nothing but a cell phone. But it was not entirely impossible that those people were there as a clever publicity stunt for charity—after all, also charitable organizations had to market themselves and in some of the homeless faces he thought he recognized rejects from auditions for commercials promoting goods indispensable to ensuring a happy family life. Why would someone choose a role like that on one's own, without pay?

Choice, that's what mattered: Making the right choice. Borut, the boy wonder of his generation, was offered a post at his department at the university when he graduated, and he accepted it on the condition that the offer would still stand after he'd come back from one more trip. His professors were understanding, he traveled a great deal, nothing wrong with that, it looked good on the resume, one had to travel to faraway lands, they had done it themselves, you were no professor if you hadn't been a professor abroad, you had to show genuine interest in the Other, otherwise you couldn't sell whatever you wanted to the Other, that wouldn't do.

From there, things went as they were supposed to. He'd been a student, now he would become a teacher, the roles would switch, he was happy, his professors had taught that no work was more honorable than teaching young minds, and the young minds believed them. To be sure, every so often one would hear a different story; on occasion, maybe over drinks in the evening, professors would speak differently, on occasion, bitterness would surface through the drink, *everything's a factory*, someone might murmur and quickly wash the words down, as though they'd slipped out inadvertently; but then, one went for drinks with professors less and less. Each to his own kind was the principle they all adhered to, and each associated less and less with people of uncertain allegiance.

It started out well. Coordinating, preparing, lecturing, grading. The production line was fast, but so was Borut. Everybody was fast, the students and the faculty. The last of the slow ones left quickly during the last amnesty, as their successors dubbed the early retirement package offered to all who were willing to relinquish their tenure to one third of an assistant professor. Borut arrived as such a third, added another one to it, and then another and one more. His pay began to suffice, the heirlooms were safe.

Right about the time when Monika began to feel that they were settled down, that their interior design fitted their prospective social status, and that it was time for children, Borut no longer wanted to be at university, he was bored by all the students asking the same questions, even worse, he began to feel humiliated. When the university became a private institution and the tuition became steeper and steeper, the students quickly became better dressed than him, no scuffs on their shoes, their teeth whiter, their tans deeper. And it did not end there. Paying more, the students had greater demands, the customers wanted their money's worth, and they brought to the university prettier and newer handguns than the one assigned to him by the department secretary together with the keycard for the lecture halls and the codes for accessing the technical equipment. Nobody could guarantee his safety on his way home from exams late at night. Of course not everyone passed, that's the way it worked, society was increasingly made up of winners and losers, more and more of the latter, he tried to get his students accustomed to that, after all, it was frequently said that the university was teaching them for life. When he attempted to complain to the dean after a drawn-out dinner about how little understanding his students showed for his methods of bringing them down to earth, quite often instead threatening to serve up a Molotov cocktail, the dean magnanimously offered to let him take a martial arts course, courtesy of the training funds, and proudly exhibited his collection of firearms. He had a bodyguard lug around his most prestigious pieces in a special briefcase, a safe investment of tuition fees. The members of the faculty sitting closest to them at the table nodded and patted their bulging chest and trouser pockets.

There are moments when one has to leave, realized Borut, and he found an opportunity in the wonderful world of copy writing. There was an unfilled niche there. The generation before him was fleeing the advertising factories for the world of artistic idleness. Those who were the quickest to pour bile on their former profession held on to its more attractive aspects: Now the big bucks, expensive bottles of champagne, and beautiful girls were their due as philosophers of transformation, critical-realist authors, apocalyptic film directors, and dark musicians, rather than as advertising gurus selling the good life. Those who missed the boat vanished from sight, to work in warehouses. But virtually all the advertising old-timers were running away, life on the front line could not be endured for long.

The dialectical turn had an effect; when the university started its production line, positions galore opened up in the advertising industry, young people came knocking on the door, but they couldn't keep up with the demands, it was difficult to learn the tricks of the trade overnight, so when Borut showed up at one of the agencies saying he'd like to do something, his PhD suddenly ceased to be an insurmountable obstacle. For lack of a better choice, the service industry was willing to employ even highly educated people.

He quickly rose through the ranks, from assistant copywriter to creative director after a few million in turnover and a few Golden Bombers, the prestigious award for the most bombastic advertisements; his clients were happy, his boss was happy, Borut was happy, Monika was happy. He got more and more accounts, more and more awards, more and more checks, Monika bought more and more shoes, and she was grateful for them, her business wasn't making all that much yet, the turnaround came later, back then people still thought they knew how to do it, that they could do it on their own, that it would work the way it had worked before, the old way; the big bucks started rolling in for human resource development companies only when everyone wanted to develop.

The excuse for his first visit to the refugee center was to do market research for a new promotional campaign ordered by the largest company in the country. From among the numerous slogans Borut had come up with for the campaign, the Chairman decided to pitch "The next pleasure will be a religious one—or there will be none." The client rejected the slogan on the grounds that they didn't see why there should be two options, the first part was almost acceptable, but they had no use for any "or" and all that, they said, and besides, it was beyond them why they should pay a sum amounting to the value of the two national parks they owned for something they already knew anyway. True, that particular client was hard to please, but Borut himself had felt that the catchphrase was too blunt an attempt to cash in on the highly successful Association of Globalists campaign—hardly anywhere in the world could one walk a block without encountering Borut's slogan: *Global Player. Global Prayer. Global Payer.*

During his all-night drives Borut often thought about what he had said with those six words, or rather, one word with three others added to it, or rather, one word with another one added to it in slightly variant forms. He knew how the client understood it—everything was global, that was a message worth paying for, and since they were Global, they were everything. And besides, any line that repeats the client's trade name three times can be sold successfully, as his rivals chuckled in envious banter. He also knew the order of the nouns in some sense corresponded to the theory of the evolution of species, when he thought about the other possibilities. He had put it perfectly. But what had he said? What did people understand when they saw his slogan?

Some of the things in this business were as predictable as in other lines of business. Others were quite different. Unpredictability was exciting. Excitement brought profit. The time was right. People had grown tired of wars, they resolved to give peace a chance instead, the time for compromise came and soldiers from opposing sides sat down to parley, the rapists and the victims, to negotiate the division of profits. The company operated on a global scale. It adapted to individual state markets. Where there used to be communism, now replaced by the more efficient capitalism, the converted communists deftly reinvented themselves as supervisory board members, divided among them the most lucrative state industries, and began to pay themselves dividends, indignant that the young hadn't yet cottoned on that the times of idleness were over, that it was every man for himself, that they were not entitled to free education and health care. *They* were fending for themselves. They had money. They didn't let others come even close. The others first muttered, then grumbled louder and louder, *if we aren't heard, let's make a racket.* The oligarchy asked its consultants what it should do. The consultants answered: You have money, you need a better image. And that can be bought—from experienced consultants. They bought it, and business flourished.

And where there used to be capitalism that ripped people off to the point that they'd had enough and wanted change, the positive aspects of the other system had to be underscored, free this and that, now you can go to the dentist without having to take out a mortgage, nobody will charge you for a stroll in the municipal park, your children won't have to buy school diplomas anymore, we will redistribute everything there is, the possibility that you might get some small share of it is not that small after all. The persuasion called for as much glamour as possible, but there was hardly any glamour left in the metamorphosed countries, the changes did not always go smoothly, on the contrary, there were quite a few scratches that needed polishing, and Borut's company could of course fix anything the new national budget could pay for, the new nationalizations were simpler than the first time around, they were far fewer now.

Having always liked traveling, Borut became the long-distance-accounts expert, going everywhere and also returning from everywhere. The Chairman would walk into Borut's office every now and then, and with an encouraging nod place on his desk a piece of paper showing the sums deposited in Borut's account and maybe a bottle of some very expensive wine, nod again, and leave. At first, Borut invited his former colleagues to share the bottles, until he began to feel that they finished their drinks in such haste not because they were thirsty for the wine, but rather because something in his office frightened them, so he began taking the bottles home, and occasionally he and Monika would open one; friends had stopped coming around a long time ago.

So now he was here at the collection center. The children spotted him and began to call out. Their broken teeth glistened in the glow of the TV screens. Their mothers shooed them back in front of the screens, then approached with their heads bent, casting glances at the two boxes. Borut looked around and they knew what they had to do.

They called the two old women, who each had one half of

the ethnic groups living in the barracks under their control. Nodding, Borut placed a box in front of each woman. They took knives from under their colorful skirts and adroitly slit open the tops. Looking inside, they smacked their lips happily. The children formed two lines. Everyone chose one piece of fruit from the box: an apple, an orange, a banana, a grapefruit, a tomato, a pear . . . Some fruit was too bruised, Borut noticed, he would have to pay more attention the next time it was being loaded. It had all gone too quickly this time, there was not enough light under the bridge, the vendors were afraid of the police.

When there were no more children in line, the adults came closer. Handing each of the two old women a bunch of banknotes, Borut said: "As usual." They nodded. They knew there would be no more relief if they used the money contrary to his instructions, they knew Borut was a major client with all the fruit and vegetable dealers, they'd heard of the time he left without a word when someone tried to sell him fakes only to see his warehouse go up in smoke in the night until there was nothing left but the stench of melted plastic. Nobody thought Borut would be capable of doing such a thing, but there were plenty of other people in this business who placed a premium on honor and a good name and were willing to root out the frauds. It was better to stick to the deal, the black market could not afford swindlers; if those operating legally cheated, they were tried by law, which took a long time and possibly came to nothing, but a person caught cheating on the black market could quickly disappear in the black of night.

Borut leaned back against the barrack wall. His head was spinning. He hadn't eaten anything in a long time. He felt the urge to go stand in the line himself and take a banana or something. But he reminded himself that this would seriously mar his philanthropic image. What normal person would give away something they didn't have more than enough of themselves? Possibly, he was only tired. Possibly, he would turn off the main road on the drive back and take a nap on some path in the woods. Possibly, some idea would come to him in a dream about how to replenish his diminishing stores. In the camp, in his trunk, in his body, on his account. Possibly. Everything was becoming possible.

He nodded goodbye and the children began waving.

The guard motioned for Borut to approach. He took him into the guardhouse. Borut saw a stack of books on financial engineering on the desk and an array of electronic devices on the wall, into which the guard nervously entered a few commands. Some of the control panel lights went out.

"There's a message for you," he told Borut.

"A message? From whom?"

"I don't know. I called my broker to give him directions based on today's information, and he said he had a message for the provider of that information."

Of course. Knowledge is a clue. They knew whom such a combination was coming from. But why would they be looking for me? I haven't—

"I only took down what I was told, I didn't understand any of it," said the guard, handing Borut a slip of paper, then put a finger to his lips and again moved his hand quickly over the gadgets on the wall. The lights flickered back on.

Borut had no trouble deciphering the senseless words. He was well versed in that code.

Come see me tomorrow at one. A good job, right up your alley. Chairman.

Borut opened his mouth to say thank you, but the guard shook his head and pushed him toward the door.

Summoned. To the Chairman. After all these months.

An invitation he had certainly not expected. But one that he couldn't refuse. It came at the right time.

4.
Libertarian Tango

AN INVITATION HE had certainly not expected. But one that he couldn't refuse. It came at the right time.

Vladimir had learned his grandfather's story by bits, by little crumbs that fell out of the old man's mouth at dinner when he'd had a few drinks. As far as Vladimir could understand, his grandfather had been the leader of some military unit in some unfathomable tribal conflict in that faraway country of his that was completely alien to Vladimir, only existing in his life through grandfather's mumblings and the insufferable dance tunes devoid of any sense of rhythm whatsoever, played on the scratched vinyl records that had survived the long ocean voyage.

Grandfather's story was always the same. It began in glory, with people waving in the streets, grandfather strutting in a smart uniform tailored from imported cloth and fighting for the just cause. Then his army lost and got lost. Grandfather ended up in some port, the ship engines had started, all he managed to do was write a few lines and press the note into the palm of a man who'd come to make the sign of the cross over those leaving, with the request that he take it to his parents. He wrote that he had to leave, but would come back for them as soon as he could. The man in black nodded, of course we'll let them know. Grandfather shook his hand, in a hurry to leave everything behind, the lost battle and his soldiers in a pit somewhere at the end of some railroad line.

He never went back for his parents, everything he heard from back home confirmed his belief he would never be seen again if he ever crossed the border. Had he wanted to die, he'd already had a chance, and he'd passed it up; it was too late now. So he went on living, drinking tea through a straw and driving to the ocean after Mass every Sunday, to stare across. He waited for things to change, and years passed. One day he received a sheet of paper in the mail with the words: *If you can't change the fate of the majority, you have to share it.* He felt he could recognize the diction of a former comrade who had fought by his side, but could not work out the message.

Then came the day all the members of his circle had been waiting for for decades. They rejoiced that their exile was finally over, now they could help their country, which needed them; he, too, gave some money for the just cause. And resolved to send his son over there; he wasn't old enough himself yet, some people might still remember what had happened, someone might still think he had to share the same fate. But his son refused to go, saying that there was nothing for him there, that his country was right here where he'd been born, that he was not interested in the squabbles of his father's generation, and that he should leave him alone.

Grandfather spent another few years thinking; in the meantime, his son had a son and disappeared, and his son's son grew into a youth, ready to travel. Grandfather considered it a while longer, then summoned Vladimir to him.

"Your father and I," he told him straight, "never got along well, but never mind. Maybe it's the same with all fathers and sons, I haven't known enough of them to say, and it's too late to find out now, but never mind, I'm not really interested. But—it's not too late to give *you* what money I have, I won't be needing it much longer anyway, and send you to have a look around the old country. Go have a look and come back and tell me. Never mind what happens later."

Vladimir was a good boy; true, he played the accordion with buttons rather than the kind with keys, and then he went and traded even that in for an electric guitar, but at least he talked to his grandfather, mixing his own language with tidbits of his grandfather's language, many young people don't do that at all, they never learn the language of their parents, let alone their grandparents, and they don't talk to their elders unless to ask them for money, thought grandfather. *Sign of the times, a lot of things going wrong.*

Vladimir nodded, of course he'd go, traveling was enjoyable, and besides, his current life was choking him, suffocating him, it was not made to his measure, more and more things were happening to him that were not supposed to, it was time to leave, to test himself, to see what he was like when not surrounded by people who knew what he should be like. He'd go.

"Do you want me to bring you back something, grandpa?" he asked.

His grandfather motioned for him to lean closer.

"Just find out if I can go back. If anyone remembers me," he said.

Vladimir thought that was an odd mission; his grandfather had a hard time going as far as the bathroom, let alone crossing the ocean. But this was his grandfather and he wanted him to be happy, he wanted things to be as his grandfather wanted them.

"Sure they remember you, grandpa, sure they do," he said quickly.

Grandfather shook his head.

"Don't make assumptions, Vladimir. Go make sure. It's better to make sure than to think that you know. Because, you know, that wasn't what I wanted to hear."

All this went through Vladimir's mind as he scrunched in his seat and squeezed his knees in the confined space and, departing in the cold of winter, spent a day seated in an airplane before he could stretch his limbs on a warm summer's day.

"You're one of us, aren't you?" the immigration official asked him after glancing at the name in his dark blue passport, and Vladimir realized that no one had ever asked him that before. Some believed it so adamantly they couldn't be swayed, others didn't care.

"I'm yours, if you want me," he laughed.

"Welcome home," said the official, handing him his passport.

Home, thought Vladimir. At his neighbors' house they would say *"mi casa es tu casa,"* but it was just a phrase, their house wasn't really even theirs, it was rented. And here, almost a whole day's flight away, they say "my home is your home." *To go so far from home and come to another home. To see everything come round in a circle. Grandpa would surely like that if I told him, wouldn't he?*

That is what he thought about all the way to the former military complex in which what used to be jail had been repurposed into a youth hostel. Vladimir had never heard the clatter of soldiers' boots on the pavement of the streets of his hometown, but he had heard a lot of talk about it, and even more about how that sound should never be heard again, every house had someone who had vanished in that noise, and if not every house, every family, or if not every family, then every circle of acquaintances; they were all marked, as were those who had done the clattering, they were also known in virtually every house. He pictured how he would feel if he had to take up arms, and his eyes welled up. It was a good thing he had been born afterwards.

He felt even more satisfied when he heard an electric guitar through the wall even before he set down his bag at the check-in desk; actually, several guitars, each in its own rhythm. Some of them felt like home, and the thought crossed his mind that the immigration officer had not been just friendly, he might have been right.

Despite feeling sleep engulfing him, he decided to fight it off. He took a quick shower, strewed some clothes around the room to make it feel like home, and returned to the ground floor, to the coffee shop.

He scrutinized the drinks menu in some doubt. *They don't have our tea. I guess a latte will give me a better boost than these European teas.* He sipped his coffee, asked for the check, and left a twenty-dollar coin on the table as a tip. The waiter's glance of surprise and quick motion as he pocketed it told him that he had far overestimated the service in terms of the local customs. But his grandfather had supplied him with such a bundle of greenbacks he felt no need to turn on his mental calculator, that gadget which never stopped working in the shops in his barrio.

"You haven't switched over to the local currency yet, have you?" an older woman at the next table addressed him in Globalese.

Am I being picked up? Vladimir was momentarily flustered, but then calmed down and smiled. *A different world. Different customs, different women, different language, different tea, and currency too.*

"I only just came here," he said. "And you?"

"I only just came here too," she said. "For a drink. Otherwise, I've lived in this town since I was born. And probably will live here until—" She cut herself short.

Your country till death, thought Vladimir, it had the ring of some slogan from his continent. But in the times and places of those slogans, that was not a free choice. There were no passports, and swimming from the island that presented homeland and death as the only two options would be long, longer than life.

"Vladimir," he said and walked over.

"Monika," she said, half-rising and shaking his proffered hand. "Won't you join me?"

Vladimir thought he would never join a woman old enough to be his mother back home in his barrio as he started to transfer his coffee cup to her table.

"Leave it there, it's empty anyway," his new acquaintance said, "besides, there are better drinks in this country than coffee, come to think of it, everything's better than coffee here."

Except tea, thought Vladimir, *are these pathetic teabags really all you can get here?*

"Seeing that you're clearly an expert, what do you suggest?" he asked, and felt immediately upset by his own words. *Am I being suggestive? Will she be outraged? Am I flirting? Will she go for it?* Both possibilities were equally bad.

"Wine," said the woman calmly. "We're known for our wines."

Not in my country, you're not, thought Vladimir. In my country you're known at universities for a fidgety philosopher who came to our country, got married all dressed in white to a beauty of ours, gained citizenship, and ran for president; you're not known at all otherwise, except by those who originally came from here. And we have our own wine. We export it.

But the woman couldn't hear his thoughts. She motioned to the waiter and said something he didn't understand. He received his dose of red.

"It's on me," said the woman, and Vladimir withdrew his hand that had gone to his pocket.

"But I'm a man," he said. He wanted to make it sound somehow ironic, to suggest he was on top of the situation, but it only came out as rather pathetic.

Monika smiled.

"Not the first one I've met. And certainly not the first one I've ordered wine for. And paid for."

Only several glasses of wine later did Vladimir realize her words had a deeper meaning. No matter how hard he tried to blame it on his exhaustion after the long trip, he had to admit that he hadn't practiced enough with their Shiraz to come even close to keeping up with Monika. The only thing that kept him relatively together was the comforting knowledge that his bed was mere footsteps away, up some stairs, unfortunately, but Vladimir hoped the railing would provide support should the ascent prove challenging.

Monika cut through his self-pity by observing matter-of-factly that the bar was closing. Nodding, Vladimir searched for some words of closure.

"There are others, though," she added.

What *is* this place? Vladimir began to wonder. *In my country—or at least on my street—a woman would never—*

Then he reminded himself that he didn't really know all that much about women. Not even those in his country. Or on his street.

"Let's go," said Monika, counting a few multicolored paper bills and handing them to the waiter, who shoved them indifferently into his pocket.

"But—" Vladimir groaned, thinking: *This is not a good tactic. A mild protest. This situation doesn't call for a mild protester. This situation calls for a man of determination. Who wouldn't say* but. *Who would say* no. *Or* where to?

"Don't worry," said Monika, soothingly. To his surprise, Vladimir felt her take his hand, as though she knew how very worried he was. "I know where. This has been my town for a very long time. A very long time, don't forget."

Is she saying that I'm so much younger than her that there's nothing to worry about?

He followed her across a dark yard strewn with broken glass and squashed beer cans.

"Where are we going?" he managed with an effort. "Where are we, anyway?"

"Back there," Monika explained, "is our Ministry of Culture. To the left, the Ethnographic Museum. Right in front of us, an outpatient clinic for drug addicts."

Vladimir nodded. I have to say something, he thought feverishly, there's a message in all this.

"And to the right?" he finally asked, feeling like a complete idiot.

"An auto shop. Closed," said Monika dryly. She paused before adding: "I've heard that in some parts of the world cars are no longer fixed. When they stop running they're simply pressed into a block and taken to the third world. We haven't come to that here yet."

You sound as though you're sorry about that. In my country—in my country we press people into blocks, it seems to me. If you're not put together right, you're lost to society.

His thoughts remained suspended inside him, and Vladimir tried to follow them, to figure out what exactly he had thought. It wasn't easy. On the contrary, it was pretty complicated. *In which of my countries? The one over there or this one here? The one I've left behind, possibly—of course without saying that to grandpa—for good? Or this one here? Where I've come to look for a new us—and it started out so well, in the beginning, crossing the border went well, the noise of those guitars went well. But—*

The identities multiplied and split up too quickly for him to keep up. *I'm drunk*, he told himself. But that had nothing to do with the splitting identities. Ever since he'd arrived he had been thinking about the possibility that he might actually be from both sides, that his grandpa might be right in saying that he's from this side here, and his father might be right in saying that he's from that side there, and they might also both be wrong. He was a boy with a button accordion, a youth with an electric guitar, a little boy terrified of being spotted on his way to Sunday school by his neighborhood buddies and of being laughed at, and a young man who had drunk a lot of wine, too much, a young man who recalled his first hasty kiss on the lips every night, and his school friend's wide, frightened eyes when she realized what had happened and that she had liked it, he was a man through whose arm a woman old enough to be his mother had linked her arm, and he didn't dislike it one bit, he was—

"Let me tell you something," said Monika, leaning very close to his ear.

"Go ahead," said Vladimir.

"There are times when one has to think. And there are times when one shouldn't think. There are things one simply can't accept. And there are things one simply *must* accept."

Vladimir knew this was a thing he couldn't think about. He *shouldn't* think about. Monika's breath was very close to his skin. His skin was reacting. It was moving. It wanted to come closer to her breath. *A new, unfamiliar sensation. No guilt involved. That thing with his school friend had been different. Guilt-laden. And no wine. A different relation of power, or correlation of power. This here—go with the flow. Let happen whatever will. Guilt-free. A new, unfamiliar sensation.*

"Where are we going?" he said.

"Home," said Monika. "Home is a refuge. Sometimes you have to retreat to your refuge."

She could burst out laughing here, he thought, she could burst out laughing here and tell him to leave. *But you have to hold on, see what you've started through to the end—*

The door gave a treacherous creak, making Vladimir want to turn around and run back down the stairs, out into the night, alone in an unknown town, to make his way to *his* home, to his temporary abode, his hostel room, furnished and made by somebody else, he'd only made an attempt to make it his own by scattering his things around, but it was still more his than anything else in this town, in this country, where did his grandfather send him to, *and why, what on earth would he think if he saw me now, I should go home, or to that room that's temporarily mine, I shouldn't let myself be led into the unknown like this, I should at least make an attempt, I'd find the way somehow, or I could wait until morning and then ask for directions,* he opened his mouth to speak, to say that it was really time for him to say goodbye now, but Monika looked at him, putting a finger against his lips.

"Shush," she said. "The kids are sleeping."

The kids are sleeping? What am I doing here? He was appalled at the state of the world that allowed for a situation like this. But he tiptoed on, imagining the situation called for it and allowing Monika to lead the way down the hallway, open a door, and, when he hesitated in doubt, push him into a dark cavern that turned out to be a master bedroom with a marital bed. *What an unpleasant word, in Globalese it's a* double *bed, it's also* double *in German,* double *is better, it's wider—*

"I don't think we need any more wine," said Monika. "And we've talked enough too."

She lay down. Vladimir tried to look over and beyond her, into the darkness, but he couldn't. There was nothing in the dark; and on the bed, really close to him, there was a woman. A mature woman, that's true, the mother of some unspecified children, if he'd understood her correctly, if this was not just another test of some kind, a different woman than the ones he dreamed about when he'd dreamed this scenario, but, unlike all those, real—he could feel her body pulsating, and the air around it moving. He remembered the song they'd sung in secret at the seminary, about a widow seducing a young priest—

"Come now. What are you waiting for? What are you thinking about?"

Indeed, what am I waiting for? What am I thinking about?

Zillions of tiny twinkling answers flashed through his brain, but not one of them sounded right.

"The kids will hear us—"

"They won't hear a thing. We have thick doors. Armored. All of them. Sign of the times."

—and the young priest thinks about his punishment, for having gone too far in his commitment and for failing to give the widow solace in some other manner, more pleasing to God, but punishment is a strange thing, since he only did what he had to do, he'd listened to his inner voice and done what he felt was right, that's what they'd sing, then laugh and disperse, each under his own sheet, with his own thoughts, in his own hand—

She didn't pull back the covers, he thought, she doesn't want to expose the bed—

"Come," she said again. "There's no other option. No choice."

Vladimir didn't share her conviction about there being no choice, but he didn't know how to choose something else. There is an invisible force that draws a person to the edge of the abyss, no, not the abyss, the abscess, no, the excess, access, acquiescence, acceptance—

His thoughts were superfluous, Monika was already holding his hand. And after his hand, everything else. There was no going back. Just sliding onward, on and on. He could feel her desire coursing through her legs. He tried to steady his breathing and think of the distant and only Madonna, of the skinny and aging pop Madonna, the blubbery demigod Maradona, anything, anything but what he was feeling—

It was like he had no memories. He couldn't think of anything else. Time vanished. A slow explosion of the universe spread through his brain. The first thing he sensed when the tremors subsided was that he was still breathing. He started surveying his body. Everything was still in place, nothing was missing.

He looked around. It was still the same room, the same city, the same country, the same world. Possibly, he too was the same, although he felt completely transformed. Lying next to him was a woman, a woman he didn't know except in the biblical sense, but she was next to him, and all the other people he knew were on the other side of the globe.

Watching the lying body, he waited to see what would start going around his brain. But there was nothing. Nothing.

He listened to the silence. It felt good.

Bending over her, he listened to her breathing. It was quiet, calm, steady. The thundering must be coming from inside him. He went on listening.

Putting his lips next to her ear, he said: "I love you."

He felt profoundly embarrassed. Whatever will she think! Teenager! Greenhorn! But there is no love without telling one's love, you have to say it, without shame—

Monika was already asleep. The words hung in the air for Vladimir to listen to. They sounded different, completely different than those times he'd practiced saying them in the quiet of his room, with his mouth pressed into his pillow.

He felt like saying and hearing it some more, but it didn't feel right, not with her sleeping. *To talk about love to myself?* He was past that now, and would never return to that time.

Suddenly he felt a raging thirst but didn't dare leave the bedroom. He had no idea where he might find a faucet, which door to try without stumbling into some child's bedroom. There was no other way—all he could do was to wait here for her to wake up, and then let happen what would. Helplessly, he looked around the dark room, finally spotting a vase with some flowers. Reaching over and rocking it slightly, he heard a tiny splash. He hesitated, but his body's needs were inexorable and making up his mind, he tilted the vase back and then quickly jammed the bouquet back in. The water had an unfamiliar flavor, a flavor in which Vladimir tasted a life like none he had ever known before.

It was new, it was good. Putting the cut crystal back down, he was careful not to clink it and make any noise, lest it collapse, this new, harmonious order of things.

5.
Split Quadrille

PUTTING THE CUT crystal back down, he was careful not to clink it and make any noise, lest it collapse, this new, harmonious order of things. His hosts would surely start turning their heads, whispering, motioning, a staff member would surely edge closer and start watching his every move, in case he made another mistake. They were still drinking champagne; it was one of those parties where champagne flowed from dawn till dusk. *Bubbles entering bladders, people entering private places, their private spheres coming to the surface, more and more things revealed in chitchat, all deals done more quickly, everybody happy with the profits, everything flowing, everyone bubbling with satisfaction. The things that happen when the right stuff is poured into the right place!*

The main host stood up in the middle of the room and clanked his silverware against the crystal.

The tinkle of glasses stopped. The man had brought a lot of money into the country, bringing also different customs, pushing the boundaries to new, unthinkable heights, it was necessary to hear him out.

He opened his speech: "Misters and mistresses!"

There was a muted buzz in the hall. In the time when only Westerners did the buying there was at least a semblance of respectability, appearances were kept up. They had manners and they spoke in their own language, bringing interpreters with them when they knew they were unfamiliar with the local ways. But these newcomers from the East, it was like they didn't care.

"Many of you ask how come I redirect financial river and settle in your funds."

Indeed, thought Borut. There are other, bigger markets elsewhere. Bigger profit margins. Cheaper labor. And yet they kept coming from the East. Forever new ones. Presidents, managers, prostitutes, security guards, rentiers. Full of power and money. As far as they were concerned, laws existed, but that was the extent of it. The machinery operated on its own terms.

"My story is simple—follow the cash flow."

The listeners nodded contently. So do we, so do we, their smiles said.

"We have big and small investors. Small go only with the flow, take what they get, smile happy. Where it flows, they not know."

The corners of the mouths of some of the listeners began to droop, only to be pulled back up again, uncertain whether this was a turn in the host's rhetoric or if he perhaps had anyone particular in mind, perhaps someone drinking champagne here, perhaps for the last time.

"But big are big because they turn things. Say no to the flow."

People nodded quickly.

"And capital can turn. Go in every flow. Not tied to country. Has no smell, no taste. So that everyone can take. Like water."

Like water, thought Borut. Can't do without water. And can't do with too much water either. The right measure. That's the ticket, the right measure.

"And also water need all living things. This in common too. Can't do without water. Can't do."

A wave of nods went through the hall.

"And if you not well. Go ask doctor. Find nothing. Doctor say, more water."

He's slipping up, thought Borut, he hasn't learned all his speech, must have run out of time.

"More," murmured the people. "More."

"So," the speaker raised his glass of champagne, "long live water!"

"Long live water!" came the splash back from the crowd. Someone close to Borut leaned over the shoulder of the man next to him, whispering. ". . . filling plant . . ." was what Borut heard. A security guard stepped up, amiably offering to refill their glasses. The whispering stopped.

Glasses began to tinkle again, the people to mingle, and the party to wind down, at least for those guests who hadn't come to do business. Borut realized that he was not the only one of the latter, there are spectators everywhere, *there have to be spectators or there's no spectacle.* Twirling his glass in hand, taking an occasional sip, he watched.

The woman began taking her clothes off without anyone knowing why. First she pulled her top over her head, some poorly-made designer knock-off. Her general appearance was not good enough to qualify her for the entertainment program. She was young, but somehow rumpled. It was spontaneous. And therefore unexpected. Obnoxious, really. The small talk died down in concentric circles, in ripples of distance. He was standing pretty close, but since he wasn't talking to anyone at the party, it made no difference to him.

She undid her skirt, then her bra, and when she stood in front of them with nothing but her panties on, with the wings of a sanitary napkin showing, she was obviously at a loss what to do next, so she started putting her clothes back on again. The attention broke, people went back to emptying and refilling their glasses.

The woman stood in the middle of the room, no one went near her. He looked at his watch. It was moving, he watched the hands, there was something soothing in that. Going backwards toward the starting point.

He looked at the woman, surprised at himself for looking at her, for his sudden awareness of her existence, of being within his reach. Loneliness was not something he had bargained for; it had never even occurred to him.

He nodded at the woman; she looked at him, then nodded back as if not knowing what else to do. He took the few steps that separated them.

"Well done," he said. "I mean, a little more practice, a routine might help, but well done anyway."

The woman looked past him.

"Maybe you're not right for me. You'd better leave," she said quietly.

He nodded.

"I'm leaving, sure. The night's almost over. Want to come with me?"

Without raising her eyes, she picked up her purse lying on the table amongst the cold cuts. A distasteful sight, unclean. But he didn't care. He hadn't eaten in three days, hoping he could manage to pull his wedding ring off. The ring wasn't budging yet, and his head spun every time he lifted his eyes too quickly.

She said: "Where to?"

"A better place," he answered automatically and started thinking about where that might be.

He gave the parking lot attendant a folded banknote and unlocked the bar from the steering wheel. She hesitated. He began to feel she might not get in his car after all; things almost became interesting. But she did get in, placing her purse in her lap, hugging it.

Driving slowly, he tried to decide whether he should really take her to his room or come up with some alternative. But the choice was not his to make, the road took him. The washed out facades rushed by, the town was quiet, the block gray except for the red in which someone had sprayed TRAITORS! on the charred remains of a burned out brewery. Next to the giant letters there was a five-pointed star.

The key jammed in the lock, as it did every night. He opened the door and the empty space growled at him. Mistake, he thought. *I should've let us go our separate ways. I've dragged myself into something I can't handle.*

He motioned toward the futon, for her to sit down. She sat down. There was no other option anyway. He tried to remember what came next.

"Would you like to—" he said. For the life of him he couldn't come up with an ending for the question. *Have a drink? Something to eat? To smoke? To see?*

She stared at him, and when he'd given up waiting for her to shake her head, she asked: "What?"

He didn't know what to suggest.

"Would you like to watch the neighbors?"

"The neighbors?"

"Through binoculars. Through the window."

The woman frowned. "No. No, I wouldn't. It's—it's not fair."

He considered her words. *Fair?*

"I don't have binoculars anyway," he finally said. *Do I have neighbors?* He couldn't remember. *Have I ever looked out the window?*

All he could do now was sit down next to her. He began to pull up her shirt, feeling tired, very tired.

"No," she said. "Don't do that."

He realized stopping would be easier than he'd thought. "Of course not," he said and rubbed his hands together, like countless times over the last few days. The ring still wouldn't budge.

If we'd agreed about payment beforehand, it might've worked. It would've been clear. Above board. We'd both know where we stood.

The woman was looking around the room. He avoided meeting her eyes, knowing he'd be uncomfortable seeing the growing unease in them.

"It's impossible to live like this," she said eventually, without looking at him.

He sighed. "I don't—" he said. *I don't—what? Live?* He was at a loss for words again, but even this much denial was good, it felt like he had a choice. "I'll clean up."

"There's nothing to clean up. That's not what I meant."

What then? He looked around the room himself. Perhaps he could see something different through her eyes. He really wanted to.

"Did you invite me because of that thing at the party?"

Is she playing dumb? Is she going to tell me I'm a bastard? That would be a different sense, a different direction; things would proceed differently from there.

"I noticed you because of that thing. Do you often do stuff like that?"

"Only when nobody knows me."

"And why do you take your clothes off?"

"To show myself. If you see me, you can recognize me."

Borut smiled. His hope hadn't been in vain. *Ha, grand words! This is something else all right. This encounter does have a different meaning. It* has *meaning. I'm waiting.*

"And do you get noticed?"

"Sometimes. They'd notice me more if I came with a gun. But then they'd also get scared more."

There's something wrong with this woman. Or with me. I don't understand.

"A gun?"

"I used to bring a gun. I don't have it any more. Different times. But without my gun very few people recognize me."

"And what happens when a person recognizes you?"

She looked at him in surprise.

"Things change."

If she hurts me, will anyone even know? Do I have neighbors? Should I attack her first? In preemptive self-defense?

He looked out the window through the dusk at the window across from him. On a TV that was way too loud, nice looking blonds of every gender were singing *gimme gimme gimme a gun after midnight.* There was no one there to hear them. The message was meant only for him.

He decided he knew why she'd come, first to the party, then here, to this room. She would leave and she might as well take something with her. *If you want to start over, you have to get rid of everything, everything has to go.* Money was no problem, but this thing . . . For a long time he had wanted to see it leave the house; it represented a constant threat that someone might get hurt. Maybe himself.

"I've got something for you," he told her. "I do. In case they don't notice you. To change things."

He listened to his own words, the sound of them, their position in space. They seemed to settle down softly.

She waited.

"I have a gun." Once these words were out, he felt that they had landed hard; they should've stayed in the air a little longer instead of plopping straight to the ground. But he had said them, there was no going back.

Seeing that I hadn't done anything with it—maybe she will.
Maybe to me.

"Silly," she said. It had a nice ring, friendly, homey. Endearing. "You don't bring about change with weapons. It's different now. Change occurs from within. In the organism. It's better this way. More effective. When you feel it, it's already too late."

He nodded. Nodding to things he hadn't said himself—there was a change there already. *Time to move on now. Make other changes.* And he knew just where to start. Her words sounded good. But they were still only words.

"Listen. Let's indulge in being a little pathetic. It could pass from generation to generation, from hand to hand. It had better be yours. For a change." *To let my children find it someday? No, please no. I'll find a better way to settle my score with the world.*

She nodded.

"I can take it off your hands if you want to get rid of it. That's what I'm here for," she said softly.

She can't possibly know, though she acts as if she did. His vision blurred. For the first time he also felt hunger, not just dizziness. His body was letting him know it lacked something. To deliver, to receive. He had stepped out of the rhythm of the world. The price would have to be paid. Too little flowed through him. He went into the kitchen and reached under the sink.

The gun was gone. It was the first thing he'd brought in, the first thing by which he'd marked this rented place as his own. Every time he entered the kitchen, he reached down there to touch it. He hadn't been checking the last few weeks, afraid he'd be unable to put it back once he laid it on the table. He was convinced it would be there waiting forever, like it had waited at his grandparents' house until his grandfather finally admitted to himself that it was over, and asking grandmother to leave them alone, told him where to look. He looked and was about to take it into his hands, but his grandfather wheezed and motioned for him to put it back. "Not yet," mumbled his grandfather. "Not yet."

He was taken aback to see such a thing kept by his grandfather, who, while still healthy, stepped over ants and shooed away mosquitoes. "This gun . . ." his grandfather said. "It was with me. This gun has . . ." He took his arm and closed his eyes. The boy standing by his grandfather's bed, holding his hand, wanted to ask: "Which war did you fight in, Grandpa?" He knew there had been wars everyone was secretive about, wars that were never discussed. But before he could speak he'd realized that the one who could answer would never make another sound.

He cried out, feeling his grandfather's hand go still in his. Grandmother came running in, looked at his grandfather's wide-open eyes, screamed, and called for his father. "This is not for children," she told him sternly. His father was confused. It seemed that, unlike grandmother, he hadn't expected death. Borut had; he had been eavesdropping when the adults thought he was sleeping, while in reality he was fantasizing about Star Wars, trying to figure out a way to convince his parents that he was old enough to see the movie.

He never said anything about the gun, especially to his grandmother. When he came over for his regular visits, she'd be waiting for him, bedridden toward the end. He'd sneak into his grandfather's room every now and then, on the pretext of going to the bathroom, and check if the gun was still in its old place. It was. And when he was a big boy, big enough to go to war, had wars not been handed over to professional soldiers in times of peace, he took a chance one time when he and his father were playing their habitual game of chess, his father finally winning without a handicap and an unknown closeness of equality growing between them, he took a chance and asked: "Have you ever heard about grandpa keeping a gun at home? Grandma said something . . ." His father scowled and Borut realized he was not quite as grownup as he thought, and neither was his father; he also realized he'd made a mistake, that there would never be another evening like this again, or such closeness as this, maybe not even another chess match. Dropping the chess pieces back into the box, leaving the white king for last, as always, his father said quietly: "I have never killed anyone. Count yourself lucky if you can say that when you're old."

He never mentioned the gun again, and neither did his father, not even when his grandmother finally died and they were clearing out the apartment and his father took forever to reemerge from grandfather's room. When he finally came, he looked past Borut, with Borut anticipating his look, waiting to look back in challenge and ask: *Anything wrong, Dad?* The gun was long gone; grandmother had fallen asleep far too often during Borut's visits, the leave-taking was more and more discomfiting, always seeming like it was the last time, and even when she was not asleep grandmother pretended not to hear Borut's goodbye. He felt it best to leave quietly, without disturbing her. On one such occasion he took the gun with him, thinking, *a thing like that comes in handy in every family.*

The gun was gone. *Who took it? How?* There were many possibilities. The guys from the south were getting ready for whatever might come, their keys never jamming like his. *Report it? No way, that would bring real trouble.* Every gun had its story, and now the child who had stood by his grandfather's bed was finally old enough to know that he never wanted to hear this one; his own story was quite complicated enough.

The last vestige of his past had left the apartment with the gun, he told himself. He had what was left for the future. He overturned the trashcan, spilling everything on the floor. Rotting fruit, moldy bread, empty cans. You could hardly tell the difference.

Nothing useful here, he'd have to think of something else. He couldn't backtrack, he'd made up his mind, he'd promised. A gun you promise must show up. He'd have to fix it somehow; with money, if there was still any left. He checked his pockets and saw that he would have to go to an ATM, a little something had to be left in his account, he couldn't have withdrawn it all.

It occurred to him that he'd distributed the money too quickly. He'd met too many victims. The action had been over-successful.

He returned to the kitchen. *I hope I don't look too down.*

"Something's happened. Something I can't explain," he said. She smiled.

"No need to explain. I know. The story of my life. Wherever I go, things people can't explain happen. That's why they're scared of me."

"All the same," he said. "All the same. I'll try something else."

She was looking at him, standing in front of the door. *Won't she let me leave my own apartment?* Borut found the possibility hilarious, though not improbable. But she just gave a little bow and stepped out of the way.

They went outside, where the dusk was lifting. Making visible everything that had been under the cover of darkness. The scrapped parts piling up in the yard. Ever since a prestigious store had opened on the ground floor, the atmosphere system was replaced every couple of days. Still, no customers came. Those who had that kind of money didn't shop in stores, in particular not in such eastern neighborhoods.

Standing in a tight circle at the corner, darkness ebbing away from them, the youths were passing a joint. Destitute women from the neighborhood would sometimes ask them for a puff. They knew times were hard, even the young shared a single smoke, but still. The guys would nod, pass it on to the old women, who would go home, pleasantly loosened, glad of the inter-generational solidarity, thankful to the poor youths. He knew better than to think they were poor; he'd bought back his car computer from them twice so far. He couldn't hold it against them too much, though, understanding the rules of the game. They at least hung out in the street, unlike their kid brothers, the screen mutants.

"Hi," he said, wondering whether it would be wise to take a step closer.

They looked at him, but did not speak.

"I need," he said.

"It wasn't us," one of them said. "Must've been someone else."

"What?"

"Your car comp, right?"

"No, I need a gun. Or something like that."

They exchanged glances.

"No can do," the leader said. "We're peace-loving guys, none of us going to war. We're exempt."

He looked at the bulges in their trouser pockets. His nails dug into his palms. Calm, you need to stay calm, he told himself. The command spread through his mind, leaving no room for anything else.

"Oh, come on. I know you take target practice at the cultural center. It's common knowledge."

They shook their heads.

"That ain't us. That's the dudes from the ghetto."

"Them? They shouldn't—"

Now they tried to calm him down, all at once.

"They won't." "Anymore." "Not for long."

That's not what he wanted to get into now, he reminded himself, not the war with the southern suburbs, there was too much of that, it wouldn't work that way, something else was necessary, something different.

"I also need money. Want to buy my car computer?"

They looked at him in disbelief.

"Unglaublich!" one of them murmured.

Another one laughed. "He's freaked out, c'est chic!"

"Get out of here. We sell, you buy, that's the way it goes, don't go turning the tables now," another one said. "You're up shit creek. We'd help out, but how? We have no stuff, no gun, no cash. No nothing today. We can give you some puff. Want some?"

The familiar taste rushed through his body. He looked at the joint, thought of that moldy bread on the kitchen floor, and his mouth watered.

"I can't. Bad memories."

"No bad feelings, that's the way things go, everyone takes as much as they can." They laughed, high-fived each other, and again started passing the joint.

He didn't know what else to say, so he and the girl walked off down the street. The Professor sat on his corner, as he did every night. With his hat on the ground before him, he played the accordion and sang. The song was about the beauties of some country, but the Professor's mumblings were so bad it was impossible to work out which country. He needed money not only for new teeth, but for surgery as well. Borut gave him as much as he gave others, but obviously not enough. People in three-piece suits walked by, spitting in his hat. Despite the stuffy heat, not a single droplet of sweat marred their faces. Borut wondered what was under their skin. Apparently he did not know the right plastic surgeons.

He threw the Professor a few banknotes. Now I'll really have to go to an ATM, he thought.

"Fanks, fanks," mumbled the Professor. Borut nodded and went on.

There was a line in front of the ATM, or rather, a small crowd. People wanting to withdraw money grumbling in unison. The machine was not working.

"The foreigners, it's them foreigners," somebody muttered. "Those westerners have ruined everything."

Westerners had not really come to the city yet. Their people on management boards were realizing that there were no schools good enough for their children in this barbaric country, where they were buying up assets and property. Like when they had bought islands in Polynesia and realized the climate was not healthy enough for their children. True, when they'd first bought them, those places were still intact, pristine, but the buyers didn't have children then. They never went there either, sending their split elementary particles instead.

Also the next ATM didn't work. Only the third one did. The thought crossed his mind that maybe only every third ATM worked throughout the country, as proof that things would get better when foreigners owned more. If anyone were still withdrawing money then. The upper crust found cash obsolete, dirty, suspect. The masses didn't have any.

He withdrew what little was left from the account. If I ever need more, I can always sell a kidney or something, and then when my finances recover, I can buy it back, he thought.

There was a hunting store on the corner. He looked at his watch, closing time. Maybe, just maybe, there'd be no other customers. Or at least not anyone he knew. Walking into a place like that is bad for one's image, bad for karma. But. Sometimes you have to go against the grain, against the current. He took a deep breath and resolutely walked in.

"I'd like to buy a gun," he smiled amiably.

The two female clerks eyed him suspiciously.

"You need a permit for that," the younger one finally hissed. "You have to be a member of an association."

"What association?"

They exchanged glances. "Well . . . like a hunters' association, for instance. Or—"

The other options left hanging in the air, they waited for him to add his bit, maybe name an association. He had nothing to add. He felt about his pockets, though fully aware that he looked nothing like a person who was about to pull out the membership card he'd tucked away in the wrong pocket.

"What exactly do you need a gun for?" said the older sales attendant, leaning in closer. A whiff of some herbal brandy wafted from her, possibly juniper brandy, something thorny and wild.

The tracking security camera in the corner zoomed in on him. He felt an irresistible urge to cough and cover his face with his hands.

"As a matter of fact . . . As a matter of fact, I don't need a gun. As a matter of fact, I'll take a compass. I've lost my compass."

The women looked at him with acid in their eyes.

"We have a lot of compasses," the younger one eventually said. "There's a great demand for compasses."

She took a box from a drawer and pushed it toward him. The other one placed her hand on the security controls.

A cough came from the door. He looked over at his companion and she pointed at a large clock mounted between deer antlers. The work of a renowned designer, frequently commended for his good influence on national self-confidence. The mechanism was imported from Asia, and thus kept time more accurately. The clock hands were moving away from evening.

"As a matter of fact . . ." he started again. "As a matter of fact, I'll come back another time. Today's not a good day for compasses."

The two shop attendants nodded as one. The old one stepped away from the controls and as one they moved over to the gun rack. He started moving toward the door without turning his back on them.

"One shouldn't give up too quickly. Let's go to the market.

We lure foreigners into our country with the promise that everything's available at our market, good and cheap."

I'm getting desperate, I must believe.

The heat was getting worse. In the pedestrian zone a child tugged at his arm. "Can you spare some money?" he said, his voice weary, his eyes scanning around for his next victim before even hearing the answer.

He looked at the boy's clothes. Torn professionally along the seams, sullied with water-soluble paints, to be quickly remedied. A uniform.

"What are you going to do with it?"

"Do with it? Invest it, what else," said the kid. "Money must circulate, that's the point. So give it to me quickly. If you stall, the value drops. I have obligations."

Coached poverty, organized, cultivated. The other kind was not allowed in this street. No room for amateurs here.

The kid started glancing around again, not at passers-by, but at doorways in which the management might be listening. His career would take a nosedive; he'd be accused of betraying business secrets and fired.

"And what would you do with the money if it stayed in your possession?"

The child looked at him with large, childlike eyes.

"I'd buy chocolate."

He must have been coached to say that, yet it sounded so logical, so real, it went with his body, there was no objection left, so he gave him a few banknotes. He was about to say that he should secretly take his cut, give some to his superiors and keep some for himself, typical third-world advice, but it was too late, the kid thanked him listlessly, well-trained, and started looking around for his next business associate.

At the foot of a monument to a poet, the Indigenos were tuning panpipes sold to tourists as a souvenir with the aid of an electronic tuner. He knew them, they'd been in the city for years. They had come overseas together with other members of the same guild, buried under unripe bananas for two weeks, deep in the ship's belly, hiding amidst the precious, increasingly rare cargo, hypothermic, and once in the port, while still stretching their stiff limbs, they would divvy up their European occupation zones. Their first earnings went toward adapting to the market, for the purchase of battery-powered keyboards whose synthetic rhythms would accompany their hymns to nature. Every city of any size had its panpipe masters, proof of being open and multicultural. Without thinking, purely out of habit, he tossed them a few banknotes, and they nodded tiredly.

Competition on the street was increasingly fierce. The better organized beggars arrived on free flights offered by airlines that made a profit from passengers' boredom during the flight, marketing advertising space and selling second-hand items. The newcomers quickly took up key positions in the pedestrian zones they had previously scouted out on street view. After a few initial skirmishes with the locals, the heart of the city soon belonged to them. Those in the section working old ladies wrapped burns around their legs and pasted scabs on their faces. The team playing on family feelings placed oddly misshapen mechanical children in front of them. Most of them looked at the ground; they were old models, their unconvincing eyes a dead giveaway, although they would occasionally manage a credible groan. The multicultural specialists tinted their skin various shades and frizzed their hair. Afro groupies did initially throw them some change, before having a group consultation and deciding that their plight was not genuine enough to deserve their engagement. They'd better wait for the next shipment of poverty and misery, more worthy of help. They went back to investing their time and efforts in the nice little oxymoron of fair trade and in organizing exotically themed cultural events. The girls generously spread their legs to show immigrants how willingly the civilized world accepted them; the young men were unable to offer similar support, since the last marketable feature of exotic cultures—preserving traditional customs by the skin of their teeth—did not allow immigrant women to venture far from their hearths and homes.

The kneelers worked in shifts. As soon as one reached his daily quota, another one would kneel in his place. The spot could not remain vacant even for a moment. The organization kept a close watch, in order to prevent local beggars from intruding. Speaking the language and being familiar faces for decades, the locals enjoyed the sympathy of the people. At first, sponsors welcomed the newcomers warmly, since they brought variety, but now the town wanted its own poor back. Where were they? Where had they gone? After having been ousted from their workplaces of many years, some attended courses on creative self-transformation and began to reinvent themselves, seeking new employment. But that made their new colleagues complain, who reasoned that operatives used to unsteady income would now encroach on their hard-earned survival monopoly. Indigenous beggars contemplated returning to their previous posts, but the individuality typical of the old continent was not an advantage in street fights. So they turned to the state for help and began negotiations on income taxation, on what percentage they would be willing to pay, but the authorities responded that the amount offered was not enough, they would have to earn much more or else keep much less for themselves, the deal did not pay, deportations were more expensive than that; there was no end to the negotiations in sight.

On the steps across from the monument to the poet, the homeless and junkies gathered. They were taking collections for booze; he gave them a few banknotes, they counted the money and were happy. There were many more up the steps, somebody had written *Happiness is free for all, nobody will remain unhappy* on the wall. The steps belonged to the church they led to, and the church people were upset. This is not right, they said, there has to be some kind of order, some difference, some reward for the effort invested. Someone, the man who first wrote in their own language, long ago, had written *We are all equal before God*, but this was no consolation to them, the man was not a member of their party.

The market worked around the clock 365 days a year without pause, the fruit ripening and rotting there, people incessantly taking away what they wanted, the fruit didn't care, it had already been plucked off the trees, it no longer hurt. For a while the legislation still allowed narcotics to be administered to trees before this procedure, but then Synthesis filed a craftily constructed lawsuit, banning it in the name of the preservation of differences, and the price of fruit skyrocketed, since the amount available on the market dropped drastically overnight—many people now only caressed their orchards, waiting for the trees to feel like relinquishing the fruit.

The two guys skillfully stuffed fruit into paper bags, laying them on the scales and throwing money into a plastic bag, all at once. Tourists enthusiastically recorded the ancient ritual on their memory cards and proffered their credit cards. There weren't many markets left in Europe where you could buy actual fruit. Ships from the south arrived increasingly seldom.

He waited until he was the only one left standing in front of the stall. Apart from her.

The guys noticed his vacillation, and one of them leaned over to him.

"Yes? What'll it be, mister?"

He also leaned closer, pretending to handle some peaches while perspiration trickled down his face. If they start yelling at me, he thought, it'll seem like it's because of the peaches. Don't handle the fruit, that'll be my offence.

"I'd like to buy a gun," he said under his breath.

The guys exchanged glances.

"We don't sell no guns, we sell bananas," the one closer to him said, laughing out loud. "You want a banana? It's good bananas, imported."

I know real bananas no longer grow here since greenhouses have been banned; I also know you can only sell real ones here, he thought. And you know where guns grow.

"No, no bananas. I need a gun."

"Bah, you don't know what you need. Or where to get it. Guns are a no-no for us. All that used to be is an old story, you listen to stoned grandmas too much."

"You new around here? You're not a regular buyer," the older one asked. Or rather stated. Borut nodded, there was nothing else to do. He could not work with the controlled supply, he bought too much, he'd also bought too much before, when he was only buying for his people.

"Take some bananas," the younger man advised him. "You need them, you have no idea how much. One? Two?"

"Two, also for my lady friend here," he gave in.

"Lady friend?" the fruit vendor asked. Histrionically, he stretched his neck in all directions while proffering the bananas for his inspection.

"Her," he said and turned toward her. She gave him an encouraging smile.

"You have no lady friend, buddy," the vendor whispered in confidence. "You're alone, I see no woman. Maybe it's just the way I was brought up, you know, different religion. But let's not go there right now, right, we ain't here for religion, we're here for business. Two, you say?"

She nodded, he nodded, the large bill in his hand was immediately exchanged for a paper bag.

"Come again when you need bananas!" came the vendor's enthusiastic advice. "For your health. They're expensive, but worth it. Bananas are an important part of a healthy diet."

Borut looked at her in despair. "Want a banana? Apparently they're good."

She laughed. "I don't eat," she said. "You know you didn't come here for food anyway. And you know all the things you tried. Ready to give up?"

The gun you promise at nine must arrive by six. Or it has to leave forever.

"Yes," he said. "I give up. I'm not buying any more guns. It's getting too hot. Come on, I'll buy you an ice cream sundae. With chocolate sauce. Let's celebrate."

She shook her head.

"No sauce. The sauce only prevents the ice cream from melting the way it wants to."

He nodded. "Point taken. No sauce."

The neon blur of a fast-food chain arched over the street. They entered.

"Two ice creams without chocolate sauce," he told the attendant in the red uniform. This is one red army that did occupy the world, he thought and laughed out loud. He felt her hand on his arm. He thought she was trying to warn him that his behavior was inappropriate for the setting, but she did not take her hand away, she left it there, and an indefinite, distant sensation began spreading through him. Their search had produced a feeling of belonging, he was ready to follow her wherever she wanted, ready to let chocolate sauce spread over everything, except them.

"We don't have any without chocolate sauce," said the red army soldier.

"I don't understand. The sauce comes on top, right? You fill a cup with soft serve ice cream from that machine, and then top it with chocolate sauce."

"Yes, but we have no chocolate sauce today. You can get it without strawberry sauce, without peach, without calcium, without aspirin, without Viagra, or without caramel sauce."

"This is insane," he murmured under his breath. He could not keep it to himself, he had to speak up. "This is insane. Why can't I get plain ice cream? What do you want to be in charge of? Why are we having a conversation like two three-year-olds?"

The attendant flushed. "Watch your mouth! Who's insane? I work for a respectable corporation. I won't stand here and be insulted!" A security guard started sidling closer in from the background, his hand on the handle of his gun. "Excuse me, sir, is there a problem?" he inquired in an icy tone.

"Respectable? What have you done with the food? You've been bragging about selling chicken that tastes like real chicken for decades! What was it that we ate before you came along?" he shouted back.

"You're a fine one to preach about modesty, coming here on your own and ordering two ice creams," the man in red muttered. Then he fixed Borut with his eyes.

"Our food is healthy, mister," he said. "The healthiest. You turn the napkin over and it's all declared. To the milligram. Local restaurants don't do that." The guard nodded, his hand still poised.

She stood by his side. "Let's go. You don't need this ice cream. And me neither."

"I don't understand what's going on here," he muttered as he followed her.

"You don't have to. If you don't understand what's going on, that doesn't mean you don't know what's going on," she said.

They were out in the street again. He stared at her.

"They can't see you," he said.

She smiled. "You can see me. And I can see you. All the right things start with two pairs of eyes meeting."

"Don't talk like that, I haven't eaten in a long time and all the things, right or not, are blurring in front of my eyes. Tell me something very simple. Are you or aren't you?"

"That's up to you. You never noticed before that I wasn't. Now you know me. You decide." She kissed him and left.

He followed her with his eyes, watching her disappear into the crowd.

A group of schoolgirls on rollerblades came speeding down the street from her direction. They had national flags tied around their heads, covering their faces. Coming to the restaurant, they started reaching inside the bags slung over their shoulders and pulling out stones. They threw them at the windows, but the windows were too far and none of them hit their target; the stones just kept falling back down, rolling at the feet of the passers-by. Give it a year or so, he thought, and they'll manage.

He saw a policeman riding by on horseback, accompanied by the usual flashes of tourist cameras, crossing himself and reaching for his cell phone. I have to do something now, he thought. I've got nothing to lose.

A long-haired man standing on a pile of books and trying out chords on a guitar without strings nodded to him. "You show them," he said. In a red beret at his feet there were a few coins and a worn-out copy of Homer's *Odyssey*.

He looked at the change in his hand and dropped it into the beret. Now he had nothing; he could start over.

He bent down. To the ground, all the way to the ground. He picked up a stone and threw it. The first stone was too light, it bounced off the glass. The second time the glass spluttered all around and the girls screeched with enthusiasm. He squatted to pick up another stone. Close to the ground. It felt good, this new, unfamiliar sensation. The sauce in his head started to melt. Alertness was approaching.

6.
Filtered Salsa

IT FELT GOOD, this new, unfamiliar sensation. The sauce in her head started to melt. Alertness was approaching. Monika awoke more slowly than usual, but she woke early, like every morning, and like every morning she looked around the room, which the first rays of natural light were beginning to illuminate. She moved the vase that was not in its proper place and watched the unknown youth by her side.

Who is this? I have no idea. He came from somewhere and he's going somewhere. Where from, where to? I have no clue. Who is he? Does he even know himself?

She didn't know. She did know, though, that Borut's study was empty, and so was the couch he'd been sleeping on these last few months. When he made up his mind, Borut stuck to his guns. *I owe it to myself.* That was his favorite phrase. *I owe it to myself.* He was the only person he was willing to owe something to, and Monika felt that what he owed had augmented greatly over the years.

She didn't want to think about those years. She didn't want to think about what had gone wrong. She didn't want to, though she knew she ought to. She didn't want to, at least not as long as this stranger was here. She knew that she'd be thinking about it over and over again, that she'd be unable to think about anything else, anything else at all, except maybe if one of the boys got something stuck in his throat and was choking, except maybe if one of the boys leaned dangerously far out the window and only an endlessly long and unstoppable moment separated him from losing his balance—

I've been happy for a great many years. Now a different time has come. It'll pass too.

She heard a door slam in the hallway. The boys were up and fighting about who'd be the first to use the bathroom, like every morning. Just a few moments more and they'd start yelling, and then they'd come running in, asking her to unlock their play machines.

She threw on her clothes and was at the door in a flash. As she opened it a crack to squeeze through, she realized in disgust that she'd failed to put on fresh underwear and that yesterday's sweat was wafting off her clothes.

Later. I'll deal with this later. Now to preschool and back.

Closing the door, she began putting her world in order.

Vladimir listened to the movements outside the door, listened, and cowered deeper under the covers.

Armor-plated, she said that the doors were armor-plated. But they kept nothing out. She hadn't told the truth. She'd lied. Perhaps everything was a lie. My God, how could I—

When he'd calmed down enough to quiet his mind, he heard that there was nothing out there anymore. Cautiously, he opened the door an inch and peered into the hallway. Everything was quiet. The shoes she'd kicked off outside the door were gone. The children were apparently gone. The wine fog clouding his brain was gone. Last night, however, was still there, he remembered it well, not all of it, but everything that happened after she'd kicked off her shoes, down to the last detail, he didn't even have to close his eyes to see it.

Water. Water, please.

He didn't dare go look for the kitchen, for the fridge. Someone might still be there, maybe she was, maybe the children, maybe—

No, he couldn't go to the kitchen.

He looked around the room. The vase was in the same spot where he'd found it the night before.

The taste of the water was more familiar now. He could drink some more. A lot more. But it was all gone.

There was nothing left for him to do in the apartment. The time spent in this room—that's okay, there's no reversing things. But going into any other room—he couldn't do that. He needed to use a bathroom, but told himself he couldn't do it here. This place wasn't—*his*. He'd have to go someplace else.

Gathering his clothes, he nervously pulled them on, trying not to look around. Not to notice traces of other people in the room, in the apartment. *I don't have the right. It's not my house.*

When he closed the door it was over. He felt the urge to go back and check that he hadn't forgotten anything—*what could I have brought along, I only went as far as the lounge, to get a tea, which changed into a coffee, which changed into some wine, which changed me, I had no idea it would go this far*—but the door had locked automatically. There was no external lock, at least none that Vladimir could see.

Where am I? thought Vladimir.

Going out the front door he answered himself: *It doesn't matter.* The thing that mattered was that he couldn't stay here. He had to keep moving.

He started walking. No direction seemed any better than the other. He went one way, got as far as the river, turned around, went in the opposite direction, which felt unfamiliar, so he changed his mind, started walking in a third direction, came to a short passageway between shops, changed his mind again and spun around. He was back outside the entrance to her building; he would have to start over. He would follow the river wherever it took him. He was bound to meet someone sooner or later, and he would ask the way.

Monika hurriedly shoved the kids into the teacher's arms, *let her take their shoes off, that's what I pay her for*, and rushed back. On the way she started agonizing: *What am I going to do with him if he's still there? He could well still be there. I never told him to leave. You have to be straight about what you want, otherwise things can go haywire.*

She ended up pressing the buzzer to her own apartment, wait-ing to see if he'd answer. *If he's still here and he answers, I can call security. He can't possibly think that he can just stay. Or maybe he does. Young people are so different now. They think they're entitled to everything.*

He didn't answer. Slowly and cautiously, Monika climbed the stairs to her apartment.

Buzzing my own apartment was childish. And the idea of call-ing security also. The guard would file an official report and then I'd have to explain how a burglar had entered without any trace of breaking and entering. The security agency would sue me for tarnish-ing their reputation, reporters would be present in the courtroom . . . I'd have to close down my firm.

But maybe . . . Maybe I could say that he'd stolen my key card? In the street maybe? He'd have a hard time proving we'd been together, I'd paid for the drinks with cash, that's untraceable. Surely the waiter can't remember every couple at every table. Not even—not even a middle-aged woman with a young man?

There were too many options, but with every step one or another fell away. Finally, only two remained: *If he's still in there, I'll tell him to leave. And if he has already left, everything's okay.*

There was a third option she refused to consider fully.

I could tell him to stay. The kids are at preschool.

No. No. Use and discard.

Maybe I should call the security guard anyway. I pay him, he depends on me.

What if also Borut pays him? He might tell him—

Borut is gone, stupid.

Gone, done, goodbye. The kids are in preschool, and until you reach the office, all you've got is in this apartment.

He wasn't there. But it wasn't okay either.

She took a shower, selected a fresh outfit, and considered what to do next. She wasn't used to returning home after taking the children to preschool. Nor were the staff at her office used to that. When she called in to say that she'd *come in a little later today*, her assistant gasped.

"Okay," she said, sounding so panicked that Monika knew she was already casting about in her mind who to ask for a job if Monika's firm was doing so badly that the boss could afford to *come in a little later.*

The message to Borut required no special inspiration, or allowed for careful thought. She spewed it out, like vomit after food poisoning.

Borut. Thanks for leaving. It didn't hurt. You didn't hurt me. I slept with a boy twenty years younger than me. It was good. It was great. It lasted all night. I took the kids to preschool and then we did it again. For as long as I could manage. Now I can't anymore. I ache all over. A different, pleasant kind of pain. I like it. The fear is gone. He's gone too. Because I wanted him to go. You should also do what you want. I don't care. I don't feel anything.

Pausing for an instant, she added:
What you did isn't right. It's not right. Good-bye.

The room became heavy, suffocating.
Dontrereaditdontrereaditdontthinksenditsenditoryouneverwill

When she'd sent it she had a moment of weakness. *Was it the right thing to do? Would he buy it?*

She got an instant reply: *The addressee is currently unavailable. Please try again later. We hope you won't mind if we take this opportunity to inform you of our special offer—*

She ran into the bathroom, closing the door behind her, not wanting any other words to appear after these, especially not wanting it to transpire that it had been Borut that had written these words, like it had many times when she'd praised some campaign or other and he'd frown and sulk, until he finally gave in, after she'd repeatedly inquired what was the matter, and admit that he had written the text, for millions and millions. Whenever she really wanted to hurt him to the quick, she'd innocently let it drop how capable he was at so efficiently helping to maintain the smooth running of the conveyor belt of goods fetishism and consumerism. Borut would start mumbling that there was no need to fall for advertisements for useless consumer goods that insulted the average intelligence, and she'd feign surprise *but Borut! Who wouldn't buy these things when you present them so well!*

Borut.

His cell phone was turned off, stopping any messages from coming through.

What's left?

She phoned his office. They never did that, almost never. Work was sacred. That was the final resort of privacy. Private messages were sent to an address that was only accessible from home. If there was something they wanted to discuss urgently and quickly there were sufficient options available. Even when they were at work. Encrypted communicators, moments of solitude on the fire escape; the toilets were bugged for sure, but it was harder to do it outside, the traffic was too heavy. In her seminars, Monika taught that the line between the private and the work-related sometimes became blurred and that it was quite normal in a four-teen-hour workday for parents to help with homework during business meetings if there was no other way. But she never did it herself. There was no need for others to notice that something was not running completely smoothly of its own accord. And should a tutor fail to show up, she'd retreat to the fire escape.

"Hello, this is Monika. Would you happen to know what Borut is doing?"

Borut's secretary was silent.

"It's just that I can't reach him. Would you happen to know—"

Speak up, you idiot! You're making me feel like a total jerk, looking for my own husband in his own office—

The idiot eventually found her voice.

"But, Monika—"

And fell silent again.

"Yes?"

"How should I know, Monika? Borut quit working here three months ago. He started his own business."

Monika thought she was going to faint.

Hang up hang up hang up quick—

"Thank you," she said and hung up. *You idiot, you said thank you, what a mistake, you should've said, sorry, I made a mistake, I dialed the old number, my, what a scatterbrain, too much work, you know how it is—*

Then it crossed her mind that her regret was a reflex, as reflexive as raising an arm to ward off a blow.

It doesn't matter. Other things matter.

Three months? His own business? He left home every morning at the same time, came home every night at the same time, okay, earlier than she did, but it's always been this way, from the start. And he spent as many days and nights at creative workshops as before.

His own business?

She called her firm.

"I'm not coming in today," she said. "You can manage on your own."

"On my own?" Her assistant's voice was close to a screech.

"You know you can manage. So do I. Let's not beat about the bush."

"Uh-huh." In her mind's eye Monika could just see her making copies of all the important files. *When a firm is falling apart you have to take everything you can lay your hands on with you.* But it didn't matter now. Everything was falling apart.

What should I do to coalesce my being again?

She opened the fridge and contemplated that bottle of wine that would feed an Indian family for six months.

She grabbed the designer corkscrew that Borut had given her after their first night together, *let what you received on the day you first opened to me open for you until death,* and continue opening to me until death, he had written on the box. Monika thought it was rather pathetic, two deaths in one sentence, where does that lead, but that's what Borut was like, he didn't pretend, as long as she'd known him she admired the pain in his eyes, she felt she would earn her place in the structure of the world somehow if she could make that pain go away, and that morning after their first night together the pain was gone, she felt she had done the right thing to forget about her boyfriend for a night and end up with Borut that evening. She liked the way he had timidly moved about her room where there was evidence of another man at every step, the clothes, the complicated books on philosophy, the postcards with karate film heroes. She liked the way he said *May I?* before putting his arms around her, although he must have known that she had put that music on to help him overcome his reserve and hold her close. It was a forbidden thing, she liked that too, her life had been so prescribed she needed something forbidden to feel fully alive.

Gone. Without explanation. Without any real explanation. Some words that don't mean—

She looked at the corkscrew in her hand and the bottle in the other. They both weighed the same.

Hmm. What explanation would she have accepted?

She put the bottle back in the refrigerator. It was nine in the morning.

This corkscrew is going too, she told herself, just as that music should go, but what music was it that time she first lay next to Borut, wondering how to tell her boyfriend what had happened, since they had told each other everything, how to explain that things like that happen sometimes but don't necessarily mean the end, how to explain it in a way that would let him preserve his dignity and maybe also hers; at the time she was certain that she'd never forget that music. But she did. She forgot it as soon as Borut moved into her apartment, with her boyfriend's things waiting in two duffel bags in the basement, waiting for a long time as if her ex were trying to say that he hadn't thrown in the trowel, that he still expected to return, they might still be waiting there today, Monika had sold the apartment without clearing out the basement. What music? A female vocal, some request for silence, to forget the pain, to be quiet.

Borut would know. Borut had total recall. Especially as regards music.

Where to now? What now?

Only one thing was certain: The children would have to be picked up from preschool by six. Borut always did that.

She had nine hours at her disposal.

What should she do with all this time? If she were at work,

that would be nine consultation hours, chargeable at the highest, director's rate. If she were with the kids, if it was Sunday and Borut was at a creative workshop, that would be one hour of talking, two hours of cajoling them to get dressed, brush their teeth, put away their toys, and do other everyday chores, four hours of cartoons interrupted by a meal, one hour at the table for the said meal, and one hour of waiting for it to be late enough to send them off to bed. And if—if that boy were still here, those nine hours would—

Phone call. *Maybe it's Borut*—The phone didn't even finish ringing the first time.

It was her assistant.

"Monika, the yellows say they can't—"

Monika heaved a deep sigh and her assistant fell silent.

"My dear, nobody can tell us that they can't. *Nobody.*"

Monika listened to the words lying in the space between them. They felt right. But she no longer knew for certain.

The silence grew dark. She could just feel her assistant thinking: But the yellows are *dangerous*! They have to be handled with kid gloves. Can I manage *with kid gloves*?

"*I see,*" the assistant said finally, too emphatically, and hung up.

I'll have to put my work on the back burner, thought Monika, until later. There are other things.

Until later. This sounded as far off as *indefinitely*.

There were two options, Monika felt. Searching and revenge.

She had tried revenge and didn't get very far. So now she would give searching a go.

Borut's communicator lay on his desk. The card was gone. The history had been deleted. Everything had been deleted. His computers were locked. He had probably deleted everything there was, he was good with devices, better than with people, people were her area of expertise. Of course she knew professionals could crack the codes and restore the deletions of an amateur hacker, but she also knew professionals would not tell her what they found. And only god knew what they'd find if they dug deep down enough in the discs.

I could smash them. That would be good revenge. A good place to start taking revenge. That thing before—that was just solace. Proof of my worth and worthiness. He'll never find out. But if I smash his machines—To think of the time he spent on them! If I hadn't trusted him implicitly, I might have been jealous.

Ridiculous, empty thinking, she reminded herself. If he had deleted everything, then they were nothing more than mere machines. They had nothing to do with him any longer.

There was no paperwork with Borut.

He did all his writing digitally. Digital texts, digital banking, digital sketches, digital postcards. Everything was on his machines. Copies, backup copies, copies of copies.

Once upon a time, long ago, before they'd even met, Borut had played the guitar. And then, later, after they'd met, when he learned to trust her ability to keep silent, when they started spending trial nights together and her ex kept calling and ringing her bell and texting her and she never responded, he'd still play it at night. By himself, for himself. But he wasn't bothered by her presence. No recognizable melody. Everything his way.

His guitar was still here, in his study. Dusty, out of tune. He'd pick it up every couple of months, clean it off, tune the strings, and put it back down. That was enough. It waited. There was a dormant possibility that it might come in handy someday.

She could smash the guitar, she could whack it against the wall. Some women did that.

But it didn't seem fair. The guitar belonged to the previous Borut, the one who didn't know Monika yet, the one who wasn't with her yet. And that Borut couldn't have left Monika either, and didn't deserve to bear the brunt of her revenge.

The revenge should touch something shared.

Monika remembered some stories about women whose husbands had paid for their plastic surgery to make them look younger and different, and then left them for younger women, for different women, for younger and different women. And the women then took things into their own hands, taking razors and—

She'd heard those stories from her clients when they got sloshed at business dinners. And they laughed so hard telling these stories they'd drool into their champagne glasses and then loosen their ties and undo their collars, allowing their wrinkled skin to show, while Monika gestured discreetly to the head waiter for the check and for taxis to be called for the gentlemen, and if not taxis, then whatever it was they wanted to finish their evening with.

All of a sudden those women didn't seem quite so insane.

It's a good thing the kids are at preschool.

Grabbing the doorframe, she banged her head against it and started to cry.

Many glasses of water later she sobered up. It's not her fault, it's not the kids' fault. It's Borut's fault.

The things to go should be the things he gave her when she believed he loved her. Everything, then. What should she start with? The jewelry? She picked her own jewelry, Borut only signed the bills—does that count? Then the art installations—she chose them herself too, and then received one for her birthday each year, and another one for their wedding anniversary. Their acquaintances used to joke that all conceptual artists in town cranked up their production a notch when Monika's special days were approaching—they might get to sell something after all. Borut was one of the very few people willing to pay for samples of skin eczema or blood-covered nails with which body artists had pierced their palms. He was willing to pay for anything Monika expressed an interest in—but again, as with the jewelry, it was only the money that was his; the choice was hers.

She went back into the kitchen, then the pantry. *Borut's collection of wines. That'll be a good start.*

She poured everything down the drain, saving for last the wines they'd got at their wedding and Borut had stored for the day one of their children would get married. She pushed away the thought that the bottles technically no longer belonged to Borut but the children. Something had to be destroyed.

She took pleasure in putting the bottles back in their place. *Let's display what's gone.* Expensive as it was, the corkscrew had chafed her palms.

She rubbed regenerative cream on her hands, and grabbing the trash bag in one hand and the corkscrew in the other, hurried out of the apartment.

She wondered how long it had been since she'd been out in their street in mid-morning. It was quite different from the early morning frenzy. There was no one around, except for a few old people slowly shuffling along pathways, gripping their neutralizers in case anyone did come along. For the first time ever, Monika experienced the desire to start saying hello to them, but she quelled it—they might interpret it as the initiation of an attack and neutralize her just in case, and then let the whole thing be explained once the security arrived.

Next to the waste collection unit the homeless man was making his bed: Monika could see him carefully straightening out the various pieces of fabric. When the residents notified the authorities that they had a person without a permanent residence near the collection unit and that something should be done about it, they were informed that in view of the number of residents in the area and the population indicators, they were due one homeless person in accordance with the valid law, and furthermore, that the social services had gone to great lengths to find one that fitted the standards of the neighborhood. But they were, of course, free to report him should he fail to keep his spot clean and tidy, not separate his trash, disturb the peace at night, address the passersby in an offensive manner, or commit any other infraction against city ordinances, in which case the procedure for exterritorialization would be initiated.

Monika felt some indefinite pity for the man, although she had seen many of his kind on her travels with Borut and some also downtown when she got stuck in traffic and had time to look around. She vaguely wanted him to ask her for money and always had a few banknotes ready when she took the garbage to the collection unit, there was always some cash at home, there were occasions when something had to be paid anonymously or when you didn't want your purchase to be traced, say in some bar where you went to regenerate your cells. But all the man ever did was watch her, never saying anything, and, feeling bad about it, Monika always put the money back into their petty cash box with memories of the days when cash was king.

She disposed of her organic trash, paper, and other stuff, and immediately regretted that she hadn't brought the bottles; no matter how necessary, vindictiveness all of a sudden felt extremely infantile.

She stretched her hand in the direction of the homeless man.

"What I have here is a corkscrew," she started cautiously. "Dulce and Gibboni for Aleksia, 2005, a collectible even the first year, now it's worth a fortune to collectors."

"So?" said the man mistrustfully.

She continued with more resolve, his reserve giving her an advantage.

"I thought I'd give it to you. Because—it doesn't belong with me anymore, and you—"

"I don't drink, girl," said the man severely.

Monika flinched.

"Oh. Oh no! That's not what I meant, that you'd be opening bottles with it. It's—Actually, it's too precious for that. But maybe—Maybe you could sell it—"

The homeless man started glancing around.

"Is this some kind of a test again? Ain't I good enough for here?"

A trickle of sweat ran down Monika's face.

"Not at all. No test at all. An act of good will."

"Cause," continued the man, "the social services people were here just the other day. Exactly—" He extracted a fat notebook from underneath his cushion, leafing through it. "eighteen days ago. And we went through all this. What I lived off of and all that. You know. And I told them that it was all by the book, food from separated organic waste, and heating from the ozone hole. And they said I can be here. As long as there ain't no trouble. And now you come here. With an expensive collectible."

Her chafed palms burning really badly, Monika pressed her lips together.

"I honestly thought it might come in handy to you. I mean,

not as a corkscrew, but because of what you could get for it."

The man quickly jotted down something in his notebook.

"Are you—writing a journal?" Monika tried to ingratiate herself.

The notebook closed with a snap.

"I write all sorts of things. You ain't gonna see it. Tell me something, though—"

"Yes?" Monika was trying hard to please.

"What does a thing like this fetch?"

She was at a loss.

"I don't really know, actually. You'd probably do best if you put it up for auction, there are some collectors who would—"

"Auction? Me?"

"Well, sure, there are also auction houses that would—"

"Take stuff from me?"

The homeless man started laughing out loud.

"That's a good one, girl. That just made coming to this posh neighborhood worth the trouble. The garbage's so-so, I wouldn't order most of this crap in a restaurant, if you know what I mean. But this—"

The sweat in her eyes was beginning to sting. An antibacterial wipe, I should have an antibacterial wipe somewhere—

"Well, I offered. You do as you please," she said, placing the corkscrew on the edge of one of the dumpsters.

The man winked at her.

"Level with me—"

"Yes?"

"You stole it, didn't ya? And now you're sorry and you're trying to lay it on me."

Monika took a deep breath.

Yes. I should scream. I should scream now. When security arrives I'll say he wanted to attack me. My word against his.

Glancing around, she saw a number of oldies out for their morning airing staring at them. All of them clutching their neutralizers.

"I'm leaving now," she said quietly.

"Cause there's women like that, you know," said the homeless man bitterly. "Them that have to do it. Cause they only come if they nick something. You like that too?"

Maybe I am, thought Monika. Maybe I am. I should give it a try. It was a comforting thought.

Maybe I never opened up to you, Borut. Not really. Ever. Maybe not. Maybe another woman lives inside me, a woman you never touched.

It was a ridiculous, empty hope.

Believe. Believe. It'll help.

She couldn't believe, and it didn't help.

She went back, re-entering Borut's room again. That didn't help either. Borut was gone.

The room was perfectly tidy and covered with a thick layer of silence. As though no one was ever meant to enter it.

7.
Arrested Mambo

THE ROOM WAS perfectly tidy and covered with a thick layer of silence. As though no one was ever meant to enter it.

"Borut! Long time no see. What have you been doing with yourself?"

"All sorts of things. Driving over to refugee centers at night, sleeping during the day, and dreaming of buying weapons and throwing rocks. It's a lot of fun."

The secretary giggled, slipping a coloring book under her desk. To bring the structure of his staff closer to his own level of education, the Chairman employed high-school graduates, if that educated, as his near associates. Staff meetings mainly employed grunts.

"Go right in, he's expecting you," she announced heartily. Like there could be an alternative, thought Borut, not even a commando squad could reach the Chairman unless he invited them, no visit was ever unexpected for him. The tables were turned on the visitors, though: They never knew what to expect. In the allotted minutes (the Chairman always offered a soothing tea or an energy drink, but it was common knowledge that accepting either was a sign of being utterly unprepared) they could be transferred to the position of branch manager in Vladivostok or instructed to hand in their company pass and amiably invited to remain loyal buyers of the company's products.

When the beeping in the armored security door ceased, Borut wrenched it open and went in.

The Chairman had decorated his office with symbols of workers' movements. A hand-wrought silver-plated hammer and sickle decorated the front panel of his desk. The plating made them look like a luxury car hood ornament. Rumor had it that the Chairman was apt to take the sickle off its mounting and start waving it about when he was in a particularly good mood. A swipe of the sickle in his office meant a million workers would be laid off in China, the rumor went on. But it was probably just a rumor—the company was moving its production from China to cheaper countries anyway.

Agilely, the Chairman leapt to his feet, just as communication training instructed, and proffered his hand.

Borut remembered the joke they used to chuckle over by the coffee machine before the place was bugged: Wherever the Chairman points with his hand, there's no more grass. Because hungry people eat it all.

"Borut!" the Chairman called out with elation. "Invisible for a long time, weren't you? So, how are you doing without the firm?"

"Better," said Borut and thought *honestly*. The first honest thing he had ever told the Chairman in all these years. And gladly too.

The only fly in his ointment was the realization that also his own response was something communication training recommended.

"It's good you came."

Good? For whom?

The long years in the business had taught Borut that the greatest fallacy of all the phrases was the one that a deal was a win-win situation. It sounded so good it was repeated a lot. The truth of the matter was quite different. If one side won, the other one lost. There was no other way.

"Listen, Borut, I have a new project for you. Big thing."

Sure. Small things are invisible from this office. Much, more, the most. The guidelines are simple.

"Actually—"

"Naturally," the Chairman interrupted him, he hated being sidetracked when he was set on his course, "also the money's big.

Your cut too, of course."

So I'd surely do even more damage with this project, which would then require even more money to fix. So I'd take on another project. The world is a well-ordered place.

"Good stuff," the Chairman didn't try to curb his enthusiasm. "A lot of historical stuff. Plenty of repressed memories. No need to waste time with presentation. We'll just draw out what's already in the people. Naturally, you'll be given a couple of experts for the regression part, a thing like this always requires teamwork."

"What do you have in mind, sir?" he asked cautiously.

Theatrically, the Chairman opened his mouth and raised his palms to the ceiling.

"Have we come this far? Are we going to be formal now? Borut, I never expected this from you. I thought we could go on talking like friends."

Go on?

"So what's the deal?" The lack of formality sounded false in Borut's ears, but the Chairman seemed pleased with their preserved intimacy. He smiled broadly.

"Good to know we're still on good terms, even after all this time you've been away! You know our motto: Once our guy, always our guy."

"There's no other choice," said Borut under his breath. And instantly thought: *Why did you say that?*

It was a phrase of postponement, not of change. According to communication training, the Chairman would now pat Borut on the shoulder in a friendly though patronizing manner and draw out: *Sure there is, there's always a choice!* And Borut, or anyone else in such a situation, should then guess the correct answer expected by the Chairman in this moment of understanding and confidence.

The Chairman gave him a winning smile.

"In the old days when you still worked here I would've said: Yes, there is. Choice, that's what matters. We just *help you* choose, but the choice is yours, we used to say. In the old days. The times have changed, though. We've speeded things up. Modernized them. And so I can say: Yeah, you're right. There is no other choice. Not anymore. Not for you. Not for me. There is none."

You wouldn't have bought that. You try to act the mysterious wise man. To persuade with words. And this speech is far from ideal. It's too convoluted.

"What's changed?"

The Chairman was genuinely surprised.

"Changed? Nothing. There's simply no more choice. It's unnecessary. To hell with it. It only complicates matters. A single option is better. It simplifies things."

"Come on, chief! I'm one of your disciples." *Sucking up always mollifies him. He never notices it.* "You always taught us that you have to offer consumers a choice. It's *important* that they choose. It makes them think they're calling the shots. That they're winning. And now you say: Not two options. A single one."

"Of course not two. One. We have to give them a single option so they don't feel they might make the wrong choice."

Borut let his eyes wander over to the office walls. It had been a long time since his last visit, but nothing had changed. The Chairman still proudly displayed a few select items from his collection of historical artifacts. The blood-stained headscarf Benazir Bhutto had worn. The scarf that had been around Jacqueline Onassis's neck on that ride through Dallas in a convertible, when she still had a different last name. The scarf of Isadora Duncan that got entangled in the wheels of her car and strangled her, the belt Sergei Yesenin hanged himself with, and the shawl Vsevolod Meyerhold was wearing when he was shot. Borut looked at the fateful accessories, then withdrew his eyes. Looking around this room for too long made his throat constrict.

"You've changed."

The Chairman spread his arms.

Arms that want to hug the world. Let those suffocate who must.

"The world has changed. I just followed."

Careful. Careful. This is no longer just dribbling the ball. Argue slowly, wait for the response, then go on. See what's hiding behind. And behind is still a ways off.

"People aren't going to like it. Choice sets them free."

The Chairman got up from behind his desk and came closer.

"They have a nice ring to them, such words. Free people, free market, free competition, free pricing, free everything—sounds like what some political party might say five minutes after winning a war. But the days of pomposity are over. Anyway—those who won't accept what's being offered don't matter. They don't have a choice either."

The Chairman turned to stare at a dot painted on the wall by his spiritual teacher of the day.

Attack now. A little while longer and you'll no longer be listening. You'll become immersed in yourself; rattle off your offer and set a deadline for the decision. If deadlines still exist in a time without choices.

"People don't matter?"

The Chairman looked at him.

Out of the ordinary. Your contemplation, your communion with the divine interrupted. This is a moment when it's possible to get through, to the quick. If it exists at all.

"When you're walking toward your office, do you ever think about how strange it is to be spending your days surrounded by people who dislike you down to the last man?"

The Chairman made an attempt at a smile.

"They like me as much as I pay them."

Borut knew what the only problem that the Chairman saw in the company was. He had everything, he called all the shots, the only thing he still wanted was to be loved, but that just didn't happen. He had the offices redecorated every couple of months, new inspiring words painted on the walls, thoughts on the grandness of their business, a calling and mission really. Initially, he came up with them himself, then, after the first few fell flat, he hired the best copywriters and only added his signature. To no avail. After every redecorating job he'd stand in the doorway of his office, waiting for praise, while people just scurried by, muttering a quick greeting and looking the other way, no matter how much the brown-noses sincerely wished they could be bedazzled by the catchphrases on the walls and could show it to the boss.

The only problem the Chairman had was people. If there were no people, everything would be all right, he'd have everything under control. But the human factor made matters unpredictable, so he stayed away from it as much as possible. It occurred to him once that ruling the world from a distance was not enough. He decided to become the president of the country at first, but canceled his electoral campaign upon being advised that he should go out into the streets and meet people every now and then, maybe even shake hands with some. He found the idea repulsive.

"Is that why you employ people that used to work for the competitors you ruined and keep them close? Before they were paid to hate you—now you're paying them a bit more to like you."

The Chairman leaned in and explained it slowly, as if talking to a child,

"The opponent's soldiers are used to fighting. Fighting a tough enemy. If they served him well, they'll serve me well too. They know how to serve. That's the kind of people I need. They do the job they're given and don't think about what's right and what's wrong. They leave that to me."

He paused.

Now comes a moment of confidence, it's just that I've known what you're about to say next for a long time.

"You, Borut, you are different. You're smart, and on top of that, you've had the right kind of education. And people like that are difficult. They always have an opinion, they're always against everything. And they can't keep their being-against to themselves. They voice their different opinions. What happens to discipline then? People like that have to be kept at arm's length. And honestly, I'm not in the least bit offended. That's just the way you are—you were born *against*, you can't change that. If one could, I would've done it already. No, you're *against*. What am I going to do with you?"

We must have just gone beyond a normal business tête-à-tête. What's going on? No one scheduled for the next five minutes?

"It's been nice chatting with you, chief. But now—"

"I see," said the Chairman slowly. "Your time's precious."

You're not overenthusiastic I'm talking too. Nobody can have taken the initiative before.

Borut shrugged.

Feels interesting, doesn't it? To live by someone else's time. That's pretty much how being a slave feels.

"So, do we have a deal?"

"What is it we're selling?"

I guess no one has ever taunted you.

The Chairman inhaled deeply and looked at the dot on the wall.

You're afraid of being carried too far. This isn't going according to your plan.

"War," he said. "War."

"Which war?"

"The next war."

"What next war?"

"The one that's coming. This is our next account."

It won't be the first time you'll have meddled in the war business. That's where the biggest money is. But it's likely the first time you'll need some creatives to do so. Usually, business is up for grabs after a war. There's a shortage of this, a shortage of that, a shortage of everything really.

"There's a war coming?"

"War," the Chairman looked at the ceiling, "is always coming."

"And we're supposed to peddle—"

Shucks, I said we. Like there hadn't been these last three months and all the agonizing before that.

The Chairman smiled in triumph.

Not only did you hear that I'd signed on. You're taking control. There's no such thing as a lost war for you.

"Just that. War. War as such. An all-inclusive package."

"Between whom and whom?"

"Between our client and . . . the others."

"Oh come on, what client would want to advertise war? That's pretty much against the taste of the general public. War profits are made in more, erm, discreet ways."

The Chairman nodded.

"That's just it. The taste of the general public. That's the problem. War's out. We have to promote it, jazz it up a bit. Give it a positive image. Underscore its good points. It's hard to decide in favor of it without a little encouragement."

He paused.

"And we have backing. Our client. The biggest client ever."

"I wonder who that could be?"

Hopeless, but worth a try.

"You know I can't tell you that. But I can say this: It's an intercultural alliance like there's never been before. But you know already. Remember one of your best slogans. I mean, one of the rejected ones."

I'm trying to forget even the ones that got accepted, let alone—

"Let me give you another hint."

Should I say "I'm waiting" or just wait? What do you expect?

"The next war will be religious or there won't be one."

My unsold catchphrase: The next pleasure will be religious or there won't be one. A minor development—next war—next pleasure. Everything's falling in place. No wonder you called me to arms.

"Oh, come on, what's new about that. All wars have been religious."

"This one's going to be different. Between believers and nonbelievers."

"I think I know who your wealthy client is," said Borut slowly. "But He's famous for having several representative offices that have conflicting interests—"

"Not anymore. The times are such that we have to close ranks and present a united front. Find common goals."

The thing is not without logic: War brings people closer to the client, as it makes them more aware of their mortality.

"Naturally, the project has a deadline, but it's manageable. Finally, a client that's not in a rush."

The right words, I have to find the right words—

The Chairman winked. "So, what do you say?"

"You're crazy."

I knew it all along, but I thought your insanity had reasonable limits.

The Chairman laughed. "He who is not crazy among you, let him throw the first stone."

I've actually thrown a stone. In my dreams only, but it still must have meant something.

The Chairman never did have real patience. Even his creatives who were paid to think could only do their thinking in their own offices, not in his. *Idea on the table, approve it, action. Blitzkrieg.*

"Are you in? The budget's the largest in history. And I'm not talking about the history of our firm, to be clear."

Borut bit his tongue to prevent himself from laughing out loud.

Compared to the trouble this project would bring, my current difficulties are pathetically small.

"We're getting ahead of ourselves a bit here. The situation's kind of tricky, we'd have to find a solution—"

You already have your solution, I'm the one who needs to find one, a way to stop you.

"The situation's perfectly clear. There are two solutions, mine and the wrong one."

If I say no, that's no solution, except for my conscience, a hundred thousand others would say yes.

"Actually, there's only one —"

The Chairman nodded. Relief spread over his smile. Finally, Borut had come to realize what was clear all along.

"—yours, which is the wrong one."

The Chairman laughed and spread his arms. He took a step toward Borut, indicating he might even hug him if that made Borut feel any better.

"My dear man! There's historic capital behind this. And capital is a beast that can't be controlled. It's not the tiger's fault that it eats the antelope."

"I'm also a beast that can't be controlled," said Borut.

He reached towards the front of the desk, felt about for the handle of the sickle, drew it out, and lifted it over his head.

"What are you doing?" the Chairman asked him in surprise.

"You'll see in a moment," Borut smiled at him.

The time is coming when it will be shameful to win a war. But it hasn't come yet.

He sank the tip of the sickle into the Chairman's knee.

The Chairman's eyes popped out and he gaped at Borut. He couldn't believe what was happening. His surprise seemed to exceed his pain. *This-is-a-mistake-this-didn't-happen-this-is-a-mistake-*

He gasped. "Why?" he croaked.

"Let's say the war has already started," shrugged Borut. "That's what it's like. You believe in it, and I don't. A clash between belief and nonbelief. Enjoy it."

He pulled the sickle out. Blood spurted in a jet onto the carpet, which was the color and feel of manicured grass on a golf course.

Or a manicured cemetery.

The Chairman slumped into the puddle of his own liquid and screamed.

What have I done? What am I doing? What was it my father said to me the last time we spoke without pretense? I'm getting closer and closer.

When the scream died out, everything was still for a moment. Then came a knock on the door.

The armor must be bulletproof rather than soundproof. Or did you get your own office bugged too?

Curled up in a fetal position, the Chairman watched Borut to see his reaction.

"Come in," said Borut.

The secretary looked in.

"Do you nee—" she began, then seeing the growing puddle, pressed her palm against her mouth.

"I think you won't be needed for a while now," said Borut gently. "Splash out a little. The clothes sales have started. Indulge yourself a little, you'll need some outfits. The new boss is bound to bring his own secretary with him, you should get ready for the rat race."

The secretary's big eyes flitted from her master's grimacing face to the stain on the floor and back. *She's thinking the cleaners won't be able to get this spot out and that's wrong, the carpet will have to be replaced—*

"New boss?" she wailed.

"Change is necessary for the business," smiled Borut. "Isn't that so, chief?"

"Security—security—" moaned the Chairman.

This word so doesn't suit you.

"Change brings security," ventured the secretary obligingly.

The Chairman growled. The foaming spittle on his lips was tainted with blood. Borut suspected he'd bitten his tongue, shamed by the pain, and he almost felt sorry for the man. Millions of Chinese would be loving this moment, he thought, but I find it uncomfortable. I'm really not the man for the job I've been offered.

"I think he wants the security guard," he instructed the secretary.

"Aha," she coyly came to her senses. "The button. The button underneath the desk needs to be pressed."

"Don't bother, I'll do it." *I'm not a team player, I like to see things through on my own, haven't you been told, haven't you read my personnel file?*

The security guard appeared in the doorway before Borut had managed to read the latest data on profits and job cuts on the screen. He came running with his gun drawn, but seeing Borut, tucked it back inside his belt.

"Borut," he said. "It's been a while. What are you doing here?"

"See for yourself," said Borut, indicating the Chairman. Lying on the floor, he no longer looked fit for that appellation. He no longer looked like a man in a position to decide who will and who won't. Rather, he resembled his former employees who now spent their days in the park, waiting for change. The Chairman twitched one more time and then passed out. "Uh-huh," said the security guard. And then to the secretary: "You can leave now. I'll deal with this. Send the visitors away. Close the door." She nodded and scuttled off. He turned to Borut: "Why did you stop coming to martial arts night?"

"I was sick of you kicking my ass every time. Every single time, week after week. A man gets tired. But let's not go there now. What are we going to do about this?"

The security guard bent down and felt the Chairman's pulse.

"Only unconscious. Shock, blood loss. Standard combo. Do about this? That's easy. I have it all figured out. Through and through. We put his gun in his hand. It's in the middle drawer. If he shoots at that coat of arms over there on the wall, the one with some torches or whatever, the bullet will ricochet. At him."

Borut smiled. "I can see you're not exactly loyal to your boss."

"Sure I'm loyal, I'm paid to be loyal. But a man's got to do what a man's got to do. You can always find another job, but another opportunity like this may never come along again. I've got it all figured out. Through and through. There's no way they can pin this on us."

"*Us*? I'm not that far yet."

"Oh, right, sure, you work from home or something. You weren't here every day to see what was going on. You keep a nice distance and you think you're not a part of it, feels good, right?"

"I'm not going to kill. If you kill him, you become just like him."

"He's killed millions. Sure, no one face to face. All at a distance. By clicking on financial reports. It's fairer to kill someone straight up. I'm only going to kill one person. The right one. And I'll look at him. I think I can take it upon myself. And I'll be able to sleep afterwards."

"I see you really have it all worked out."

"I do. Hanging around in the security booth leaves you a lot of time on your hands for philosophy. And besides, it's not like I've come up with anything new. I hear managers in the developed world are systematically getting shot by their security guards, it's all organized. Nobody else can get close enough to them. It's the start of the new revolution."

"Then I don't want any part in that either. The power lies in not using power."

"Borut, you're too smart for your own good. I'll think about this when I have the power not to use it."

Borut shrugged.

"You have what matters. Choice. You have a choice. Are you sure you're not making the wrong choice?"

The security guard gave him a look of exasperation.

"You got me, Borut. I've kicked your ass one time too many on fight night. You're getting your own back. What do you think?

What would you choose?"

"I've made my choice already. I'm leaving."

Disappointment spread over the security guard's face.

"If you think so."

"The secretary will tell everyone what happened."

"No, she won't. She's not that stupid. She's here all the time. She knows what's going on. She's one of us. She'll tell the same story as me: You two had a fight, you defended yourself with the sickle, it's got your fingerprints on it, the Chairman tried to shoot you, there'll be just his prints on the gun, and he shot himself, the bullet ricocheted and all that. By the time I came it was all over. Less than a minute between the button being pressed and my arrival. Commendable, but too late. He had already fired the shot. The autopsy can't tell the time of death to the second. Yeah, sure, you'll have to give a statement, but you know now what statement to give. Self-defense. And then you panicked and ran away. That's understandable. You'll be in the papers, but you won't go to court. It'll all add up. Everything's recorded here, the phones are all bugged, there are motion-sensitive cameras in the offices, everything. Everything except his office. You know, the right to privacy. Somebody has to maintain it, so that the distinction can be known."

Borut smiled. When you were throwing me on the mat it didn't show that you think so many moves ahead.

"A man's bleeding here while we're having philosophical discussions."

"Let him. Let him bleed. Flow is good, he used to say, back when he still spoke to us."

"If you kill him, the next one in line will take his place. They're waiting."

"They'll be fewer if they know what lies in store. But let's drop this. We'll deal with this when it comes. These times we live in, you just take one day at a time."

"Listen, we can't stand here chatting while he's bleeding."

The security guard gave him a conspiratorial wink.

"Bleeding, bleeding! Are you afraid he's going to bleed to death? You wouldn't like that, would you? Then I wouldn't have to make any choices. You would take the blame then—sorry, the credit."

That's true, if I wanted to put a stop to it, I should have struck elsewhere. I thought he'd change his mind if he felt pain. Naive, indeed.

"Not likely. It's a superficial wound. You know I never could throw a good punch. The old man's not used to pain, that's why he blacked out. You'll have to make your own choice."

"Choices, quick choices, that's your strong point, Borut. Except in fighting. There you were afraid. Of yourself. Of what you might do. So you waited to see what the others would do to you. But you're quick in business."

"Not anymore. Now I'm slowly making up for my rash choices."

The security guard spread his arms.

"If that's the case, we're done. It was nice chatting to you. You'll find out later what choice I made."

Borut looked at him for a long time.

"I don't envy you one bit."

The security guard stroked his face.

"That's what I've been telling you. Like in fighting. Afraid. Of what you'd do. Of hitting too hard. Off you go now, Borut. It'll be easier for me on my own."

Borut nodded and went to the door.

"Borut?"

"Yes?"

"You do know it'll be the same whether you're here or not, right? Self-defense? The sickle in the knee? The shot?"

"Something won't be the same."

"What?"

"I won't be here."

He stepped outside and softly closed the door behind him. He stood there for a while, listening for the shot.

It's armored. But things like that can still be heard, can't they?

Then it suddenly seemed pointless. He walked past the secretary, nodding to her.

"There are other, better jobs," he told her.

"I know," she replied. "But they're all taken."

"That might change. People come and people go. Many things can change."

"I'm glad to hear that," said the secretary seriously. "That's what I'm waiting for. Change."

She motioned toward the door.

"Will the things in there—sort themselves out?"

"They will," said Borut. "Hopefully, to your liking."

"I hope so too. That's another thing I'm waiting for: For things to sort themselves out to my liking."

They nodded to each other and Borut left. There was no rush. They would not find him any time soon. There was still time. He was careful of the traces he had left. There weren't many. That would all come in handy now.

The air in the street was sticky and burning, it felt like he'd stepped into one of those soft drinks advertised in neon.

8.
Paralyzed Quickstep

THE AIR IN the street was sticky and burning, it felt like she'd stepped into one of those soft drinks advertised in neon. The street was congested, stuck together, swift as a torrent. She watched the people. They were caught in a current. Flowing down the street. Seated under Plexiglas awnings. Eating their Hunger Burgers in silent concentration. *Every bite counts. The mechanical rhythm of the jaws soothes. Balancing out the weight of the world. The persistence of a machine. On and on. Faster. Faster. Stronger. Stronger. Who stands. Who falls. All intertwined. All ordered. An influx of strength. You become liquid. You go on, finding a way. By changing your form enough you can bypass any obstacle.*

A tap on her shoulder jerked her out of the flow. Flinching, she turned around and flinched again.

"This can't be," she said. "You. *You.*"

"Me," he said.

"Don't you know that even in a city of only half a million it's impolite to accidentally run into the woman you slept with the night before in her moment of weakness?"

In her moment of weakness. How melodramatic. They could make a television series with a hundred low-budget episodes about that moment. And the same thing would happen in every one of them.

"It's not exactly accidentally," said Vladimir. "And I—"

I could add and I don't exactly recall any weakness, at least not on your part, but I won't. Despite my weakness, I'm too polite.

"No? Were you waiting for me outside the door? To come

85

back? Did you follow me to town?"

"Actually—"

"Yes?"

"Actually, yes."

"Why's that? Have you fallen in love?"

A long pause.

Is he thinking about it? Doesn't he know?

"No. I got lost."

Borut would've said that's the same thing.

Once.

What does he think now?

Enough of this Borut this, Borut that! Why do I keep thinking about him? Traitor. He's gone. I should throw him into some deep pit inside me and cover him with rocks and silence.

She looked at the boy standing in front of her. He was smiling in embarrassment, his hands shoved deep into his pockets, trying to mask that he was shuffling with uncertainty.

He looks even younger by day. Oh my.

"I didn't know which way to go. I tried left and right and I always ended up back in the same place. So I said to myself—I'll just follow her. When I saw you."

Oh my oh my oh my. Bare-breasted liberty leading the people.

"So—what now? Where to now? Where would you go if you knew how to get there?"

"Well, to the hostel, to take a shower. And then—"

The pause was too long.

"And then?"

"I don't know. I don't know anyone here. Anyone but—"

Monika saw it coming: *you.* She didn't want them to bond any further.

You've served your purpose. This is not a relationship, this isn't love. This is revenge. The pleasure of revenge, not the pleasure of pleasure. Go away now. Get lost.

"Look. I'm busy."

That's interesting. I didn't go to work but I'm busy. Busier than ever. But—what is it that I'm actually doing? I'm in the street. Why? Am I trying to find Borut? Am I trying to erase Borut?

Vladimir took a step back.

When I was told "I'm busy" that meant: Go to your room. It's not for your eyes. Or your ears. And I'd do as I was told.

"So I can't come with you," he said.

"No, you can't."

He nodded.

"You can, however," she continued, "walk with me part of the way."

What am I saying! Walk with me? What on earth for? And where am I going anyway?

She started walking in the direction of the city park. The last time the city administration put it up for auction, it didn't reach the reserve price, so admission was still free, it still teemed with people. Old people walking their companions, nannies with babies, people who'd lost their jobs, people who'd never had jobs.

"Busy with what?"

Right: Busy with what?

"Listen, be honest: you have nothing to do, and you want to do it with me?"

Seriously, Vladimir shook his head.

"I do have something to do."

"Well, let's hear it."

"It's my grandfather who sent me on this trip. My grandfather is—"

Monika raised her hand.

"Are we going all the way back to the civil war?"

Actually, we should, if I understand this correctly.

"I thought you wanted to hear."

I've hurt his feelings now. What am I doing with him? He's young. Girls are his style, not women. Long sessions on park benches, what kind of music do you like, the meaning and purpose of life and that sort of thing. And I'm a woman who could be, in terms of experience, his mother.

"Sorry. Go ahead, tell me."

Vladimir felt tongue-tied.

"In a nutshell," he said dryly. "My grandfather is from this part of the world."

Back to the roots. To see where your milk flowed from. A frequent occurrence. The more we move around, the less we know where we are. And when you don't know who you are, you look around to see who you might be.

"And he wants to know what his birth house looks like now. Do you have the address?"

"I don't have any address. And besides, their house was burned down."

"Burned down? How come?"

"It was wartime."

"Wartime?"

"After the war."

"After the war? Which war?"

"I don't know," Vladimir admitted.

Monika frowned.

"Oh, come on. There haven't been that many wars. One only every couple decades."

"I don't know. My grandfather never spoke about that. He wouldn't."

It's true, on the other hand, that I never asked. I didn't want to. He waited for me to ask.

"He wouldn't talk about it? What did he talk about then?"

"About my coming here. And seeing if anyone still remembers him."

"I see. And? Have you found anyone?"

"I haven't started looking yet. I don't know how to go about it."

"You don't? That's easy. You stand outside some home for the elderly and start asking those who come teetering out: Excuse me, would you happen to remember my grandfather? No? What a shame, you can die now. Next! What's your grandfather's name anyway?"

Vladimir started laughing. "I don't know."

"You don't know your *grandfather's name?*"

"I don't know his real name. He changed his name."

"Why?"

"Allegedly they were after him, to kill him."

"Kill him? Why?"

"I don't know. Apparently he did something they thought was wrong."

"Wrong?"

Yes, doing something wrong was possible. Actually, quite likely. Though—. She taught just the opposite at her workshops: You haven't done anything wrong. Ever. You're all great. The best workers, the best company. Personal growth is what matters. The ego has to be whole and strong, or else business fails.

"So the others thought, was what he said."

"But it wasn't wrong?"

I don't know. I don't even know what it was. And if I knew— would I know what was right and what was wrong?

"He says not."

"Then he'll die peacefully. Why does he want validation from people who remember him?"

"I don't know."

"Aha. So he ran away?"

Vladimir shook his head.

We don't run away.

Wait. Wait.

What did you do?

"Don't be ashamed," said Monika. "When things go wrong—"

What a good phrase! When things go wrong. I have to remember that. Not: You did wrong. Not: Your boss thinks you did wrong. Things went wrong. Unaccountability.

"—a lot of people run away. People in the West and in the East. Trotsky ran away. Also the Dalai Lama ran away."

"Hitler didn't run away."

"Hitler was smart. He knew he had nowhere to run."

Hitler didn't run away. That's what the men that used to meet at grandpa's house would often repeat, Hitler didn't run away. And then they'd argue. That he did run, but had nowhere to go. That he didn't run and that it was the greatest victory for a soldier to choose for himself when to end it. And then someone would draw a gun and say: You can choose too. And then they'd be silent. And then grandpa would start playing those awful records again.

"So you think that it wasn't his choice to stay? That he couldn't have run? You said yourself that many ran away."

"He was in more than two minds those final days, they say.

Choosing between poison, the rope, and a bullet. And he chose. To poison the women and the children, and put a bullet through his head, that's the right way to go for a soldier."

If you make a mistake that you can't fix, you have to assume responsibility for the consequences.

No.

He would've done better to run. At least those children would've lived.

The kids. I mustn't forget about preschool. I'm not used to that, I could forget.

"You think it's wrong to run away? When everything goes wrong?"

Monika stared at the ground.

"What was it that went wrong?" she said softly.

"Well, he'd done a great deal of harm," replied Vladimir, bemused. "Hadn't he?"

A great deal of harm?

Then she pulled herself together.

"Right, you're talking about Hitler."

"Who else?"

Should I tell him whom I've been thinking about? What came to my mind?

I can't tell him stuff like that, I don't even know him, except—

Except in the biblical sense.

But who can I tell?

Who do I even know? I mean really know? Not even him. Not even Borut.

Did he run so that he wouldn't do something he'd—

Stop it. Stop it.

But you know it's possible. You can see. You were wrong. In reality he's different. You don't know him.

"You don't know him."

Vladimir laughed.

"Sure I don't, I don't know anyone here. Anyone but—"

Monika reached out.

Stop him, shut his mouth without touching him.

"Don't speak."

No intimacy. Not anymore. There has been too much.

Vladimir stepped back.

He doesn't want me to touch him. He's embarrassed.

Fine.

"I won't speak if——" said Vladimir. And fell silent.

"If—what?"

He shrugged.

"You can speak. So, do you know our language then?"

Vladimir hesitated.

"I know a little. Just a little."

"Why are we speaking Globalese then? Go on, say something."

Vladimir cleared his throat and straightened up.

"I bid you a good day. My grandparents come from these parts. I trust you are feeling well."

Monika clapped her hands enthusiastically.

"Great! It's so—archaic. Your accent! Like it's been stored in a deep freezer for decades. And your manners! They don't make them like that anymore. It's as if you were raised in a monastery."

Actually, I was, but I'd rather not go into that now—or ever, actually.

"Thank you."

How does that song go, about not needing to say thank you? If you're friends with someone? If you're in love? If you've slept together?

"You're welcome."

An exchange of courtesies. To formalize the relationship. It's safer.

"May I ask you something now?"

"Go ahead."

"How was it last night?"

Monika smiled. "You want advice?"

I'm giving advice for free? I must be way gone. Okay, sleeping with someone, that's understandable. A lot of people do that. Also with people they don't, what's the expression, that they're not in a relationship with. So we've come this far. But giving advice for free?

Vladimir nodded.

She looked at him. Could he be joking? This guy's really straight out of a telenovela.

"It was—nice. But. When you're doing it, it should really be the only thing on your mind. And you, you have everything on your mind. Like you're trying to sort out the world. That's fine, but not at that time. In that moment, you have to think only about yourself."

Or rather—me. And you were thinking about all sorts of things. I saw you. I could feel it. But don't worry. It was nice.

Vladimir nodded.

"That's what I'm learning to do. That's why I came here."

"To think of yourself?"

"Well—to learn to think of myself."

"That's a good one. Who did you think of before? Before coming here?"

Wrong things. Well, of course, of that hasty kiss and my school friend's large, frightened eyes—

"I didn't think of who I should have. Or so I was told. Him."

"Your grandfather?"

"No. God."

"God? But you're not a priest—" *They get paid to think of God, or how does that—*

Actually, I'd rather never go into that again.

"I was supposed to become one, actually."

"And—how come you didn't?"

You can see for yourself.

"I didn't believe. I guess that must've been the reason."

She started laughing.

"Maybe you're too young to believe. Maybe you should wait a little longer for God to show himself to you."

"You don't wait for God. He waits for you."

Monika frowned.

"*He.* It bothers me that it's always *He.* It would feel closer if it were *She*, I might even listen to *Her.*"

Religious feminism? That's something the market needs—

Vladimir smiled.

"That was one of the first things they taught us."

"What? That it's a *He*?"

"No. That people come up with all sorts of excuses for not believing. Until it happens."

What a handy explanation! Things just happen. And we accept them. Without destroying the family wine collection, without sleeping with the first person we meet, and without going for a walk in the park with him. Acceptance, a great power. The greatest of them all.

She stopped.

"Wait. This bench—"

I used to sit on this bench, years ago when I still had time to come to the park, and I'd sit here and think about the similarities between my boyfriend and Borut. And the differences between them. The bench is just as I remember it. The same. I remember it well. But I can't remember their similarities. Or their differences. Or my boyfriend. Just Borut.

"Let's sit down please. I'd like to—I'd like to take a break."

Vladimir looked about.

"Is something the matter? Would you like to go on?"

"No. It's just that—How come some of the trees are so bright green and others look sort of—tattered?"

Monika laughed.

Tattered! This boy was seriously funny!

"That's easy. Some of them are natural, and others are artificial."

"Artificial? The worn ones are fake?"

"No. The worn ones are natural."

Love is like that, isn't it? The natural type grows, develops in its own direction, and then withers. The fake type remains forever green.

She hated the comparison.

Cheap. Borut would find it cheap.

She sat down, motioning for him to join her. She left her arm extended a bit longer, so that he wouldn't sit too close. He didn't. He sat on the far end of the bench, looking at the trees.

Then he turned to her.

"What do we do now?"

He can't think we're going to kiss, surely?

"How about getting something to eat? I'm hungry."

Vladimir nodded.

She took out her communicator and ordered a mixed Mexican takeout for two. When the screen flashed with a text informing her that it would be delivered in seven minutes, she realized that she had failed to conduct the standard culinary negotiations.

"Wait, do you eat meat?"

"Sure I eat meat," said Vladimir, surprised.

"And vegetables?"

"And vegetables. With meat, sure."

Monika laughed. *I won't ask him about the E numbers, the fats, the psycho-stimulants, preservatives—it's too complicated for him as it is.*

Uneasily, Vladimir slid even further toward the end of the bench. "Is everything okay?"

"It's okay," she said, smiling. "It is. And it's coming. The food, I mean."

She typed a larger tip than usual into the terminal of the boy who came running to them through the park carrying a heater bag.

"Keep the change. For a coffee," she said out of habit.

The boy laughed.

"What coffee! I'm saving up whatever I can for a trip to Mexico."

"You like it that much? You have the right job then."

"I don't know, I've never been there. But the human resource department says that the staff need to have the right education. Whoever's not been to Mexico will have to leave in a year. Leave the company, I mean. And I like delivering Mexican food. It's light. Chinese is much heavier."

Could they be one of my clients? It sounds a bit odd, this idea. But it's not without logic. We also eat cultural stereotypes with our food. If you're selling Mexican food you should be wearing a sombrero and a long mustache and know some Spanglish, at least a few steps of Mexican dances . . . providing an integrated service.

"Have a nice trip," she said. Vladimir had already undone his wrapper and sunk his teeth into the contents. *Hungry.* A greenish juice trickled down from the corner of his mouth. Ill at ease, he wiped it with the back of his hand and started feeling about for the paper napkins printed with ads and lifting them to his mouth. *He saw me seeing it.*

"If I go on the trip, it'll be nice. Hasta la vista," the delivery boy said happily and rushed off. Then it dawned on him and, stopping in the middle of the grass, he shouted in their direction:

"Thank you! Gracias!" Monika waved him off. *Who could have done such a sloppy job teaching them human relations.* She tucked a napkin in her pocket, *I must offer them my training program.*

The thought suddenly seemed odd.

Am I still in the business? What time is it?

They ate greedily, hastily, relentlessly. Crumbs slid between their fingers, falling on the ground. Birds began circling around them, then ventured nearer to their feet, picking at the remains.

They're hungry. If they were artificial, they wouldn't be hungry.

A group of teenage girls came down the footpath. Their ankle bracelets and piercings clinking, they giggled, whispered among themselves, and kept glancing at Vladimir. As they approached, their gait slowed down.

They want to do something, but don't know what.

Then one of them stepped out of the line, right in front of them and arched her body. The tattoo around her bellybutton was of the mandala made by one of the ex-presidents before his self-immolation.

"Hola, macho! Qué tal?" she said.

Vladimir shuddered as if he'd tripped over an electric fence.

Hey, don't panic. They haven't spotted you for who you are. Their language is the language of Mexican soaps. They don't know how to approach a guy in their own language.

"Have we met before?" he answered in Spanish. Naturally, the girl didn't understand.

"A foreigner," she called to her posse over her shoulder. They screeched with enthusiasm.

She continued in Globalese:

"Why are you hanging out with that auntie? Need a momma?"

Perplexed, he turned to her. Feigning disinterest, Monika began gathering up the garbage and said: "She asked you."

He said nothing.

He's deciding which language to use. His? Theirs? Something in between?

"We know a nice place for fun things here in the park. Wanna come?"

What are they going to do? Smoke pot? Play videogames?

Experiment with new chemicals? Or—

What does it matter, I don't fit into any of the combinations.

He's looking at me again.

Like a child. I have two of those at home already. Well, no, in preschool. At the moment.

She smiled at the girl: "You can take him, I'm done with him. You need him more, all alone all the time, isn't that so, you poor little thing, Mommy and Daddy gone all day, they just leave you some money and that's it, right?"

"Hey, grandma, you're awesome," said the kid disdainfully. "Just watch your veins. So they don't get clogged."

"You seem totally clogged to me," replied Monika sweetly.

The girl snorted angrily, but couldn't think of a comeback. Her friends chuckled nervously.

"What do we do now?" said Vladimir uncertainly.

"You—whatever you want. I'm going to work. And you—can go with them. As you wish. You choose."

"What do you think would be right?"

"Hey. I can't advise you on this, really."

I'm an interested party.

Interested? In his leaving? Or staying?

I'm going to work I'm going to work I'm—

A safe harbor. When everything goes wrong you can always go to work. There you make the choices.

Unless my assistant has already made copies of everything. And transferred them to some dormant company of hers.

"Come on, let's go," the girl spoke up again. "We can't wait forever, youth doesn't last, you know."

Vladimir looked to Monika again. She nodded to him. *Each to his own.*

"Bye."

"See ya," he said uncertainly.

Hmm. Again? That's all I need.

"Sure," she said and started checking out something indefinite on her communicator.

She followed the bevy with her eyes. One of the girls was

already grabbing at Vladimir's hand and he was trying to hide it behind his back. *Prey. They're going to tear him apart and eat him alive.*

Monika reminded herself that it might be envy speaking and tried to distract herself by pressing all the lunch wrappers into a ball.

I feed him and he leaves me.

The thought was too banal again.

Again. Borut would find it cheap.

Let him go. Things tend to sort themselves out if the odd one out leaves.

She looked at her feet. The crumbs were gone.

Should she go home again?

Don't go. There's nothing there, not even his message. Stay.

So she stayed in the park. Looking at the clouds. The clouds that used to be wonderful.

Real? Fake?

Monika felt she might be running a tad late for preschool. *Does it close at six or half past? This is Borut's domain. How should I know?* She had to show her pass to the armed guard watching the playground that led to the building, because he didn't know her. Guard duty had to be paid extra, but the parents' vote was unanimous: Money well spent, the children were safe, and those outside were unable to get into the playground.

She was relieved to see that there were other parents coaxing their children into their cars, but the teacher was nonetheless very cold to her when she saw her.

"You're a bit late," she said.

"I'm sorry. I couldn't—"

I couldn't make it sooner I couldn't find the keycard to the apartment I couldn't find the car keycard I didn't know there'd be so much traffic I couldn't find a parking place—

"—I'm not used to—"

The teacher nodded.

"I know. That's why I'm glad you finally came. The children are usually picked up by your—"

She waited for Monika to realize it was her turn.

"Husband," she said.

"Thank you. Protection of personal data, you know. We get your pictures and contacts on the enrollment form, but not your interpersonal relationship. So—"

She paused again. Has something happened to the children?

"Excuse me, are the boys okay?"

"Sure they're okay, we have double security control and we film everything happening in the classroom, you signed for it."

Signed for it?

"Or your—husband did. It's routine procedure. We can't make surveillance recordings without permission. And you can't put your child in preschool without surveillance recordings. Of course, there's always private childcare. But childcare without a camera, you know, if I had children, I'd never— Sorry. I got sidetracked a bit. So, I'm so glad you decided to drop by. I understand how it is, a lot of women nowadays hold jobs that prevent them from spending much time with their children. And fathers, of course, play a specific role in a child's upbringing. Which they do well. For the most part. But—"

Monika recalled the moment before she banged her head against the door.

Ohmygodohmygodohmygod. What if Borut—

"Excuse me, did Borut do something?"

The teacher gave her a look of incomprehension.

"Borut? Aha. Your husband presumably. Do something?"

"Wrong. With the children, I mean."

Monika suddenly felt understanding wafting toward her from the teacher. *I told you fathers couldn't be relied on,* her swollen benevolence seemed to be conveying.

"I see. No, no, of course not. We would have reported that immediately, you see. To the services. And you, of course. We've had cases, you know— No, what I'm saying is that there are certain things men somehow just can't, how shall I put this adequately— The biological connection is nonetheless something that, you know what I mean, nine months sharing the same body, that's no small matter. It's been scientifically proven— Well, in short, I feel that it's right that you came. Because—"

Monika waited before realizing the teacher was expecting encouragement again.

"Because?"

"—because there are certain things regarding which men just cannot compete with us. Someday, maybe. It may happen, I'm not saying it won't, it's possible. I'm not against progress, or science and all that. But not for the time being. And I'm talking about now. For now, it's still the mother that's number one, no matter what the man may imagine. And they do imagine, you know. Yes, they imagine all sort of things. I mean, I can't say anything against him, your man. Punctual, nice, the children talk about him all the time. Positive identification, good for boys, more radical people might say—indispensable. Oh, well. He's dropped out of the anti-addiction therapy sessions, but that's just the way it is, freedom of choice, it's optional anyway."

"Anti-addiction therapy?"

"Preventive, sure. But, how shall I put it—it's never too early. I could show you some statistical data. I could also tell you some stories, of course, if we hadn't all taken a confidentiality pledge. We have that here, but in private childcare, god knows. You hear all sorts of things. It's not easy, I can tell you this much, this job is not easy."

Again, Monika waited. There was no real cue.

"I understand," she finally offered.

"I'm glad you do," said the teacher. "Because, you know, that's not very frequent. It's necessary to understand, but it's not frequent. Take fathers, for example. They pay and then expect to see it done without any difficulty. Because they've paid. While we women—"

"Understand difficulties?" ventured Monika.

"Exactly. That's why I'm glad you came. Because I believe we can find common ground. Real common ground."

She took Monika's hand and pulled her closer.

My god, what's going on here? If you've hurt the kids, Borut, I'll find you no matter where in the world. There are killers for hire, your boss, your ex-boss is sure to know some, I'll work it out, we'll make arrangements, the kids will never know, ever, anything—

"Because we really can't rely on these men, you know," the teacher whispered in her ear.

Monika's eyes welled up. At that moment her younger son came running around the corner.

"Mommy," he said and stopped, surprised. "Where's Daddy?"

"I don't know," said Monika without thinking and received an understanding nod from the teacher. She let go of her hand and motioned to the little boy.

"Go get your brother. You're going home."

"Yeah," said the little boy. "Everyone's gone." And he ran back around the corner.

"They're good boys, there's no denying that," said the teacher. "But they do have, how shall I put it, their obsessions. The younger one spent the entire day today drawing Angels of Vengeance. The whole day! I don't know what you did yesterday—"

"Nothing special," said Monika as the silence grew, and was shocked by her own words. *Nothing special?*

"So then I told him: Do you think you could draw something that's not an Angel of Vengeance? And then he did draw something else. It can be done, you know."

The silence dictated the question: "What did he draw?"

Triumphantly, the teacher produced a drawing of an indistinct monster with huge terrified eyes.

"What is this?" asked Monika.

"Why, a baby Godzilla, of course," said the teacher, taken aback, giving Monika a nasty look: "You don't spend an awful lot of time with your children, do you?"

"Well—" said Monika, noticing with relief that the boys had put on their shoes in the meantime. *On their own. I didn't know they could.*

"We're ready, Mommy!" they proudly yelled.

"They're ready," she announced to the teacher. The teacher nodded irritably, *what a shame, and we were just having such a nice chat!*

"Thank you for your effort," she added.

What should I say to her that'll make her happy?

"Don't mention it, all in a day's work. I have to. But you

were late."

"My apologies again. Is there an extra charge?"

The teacher waved it off.

"The management will see to that. You know I can't accept cash. Where would that get us!"

Monika had no idea. "Thank you," she said again, and the teacher waved it off again.

"I see," she said softly, "that the man's in charge of things in your household. But I tell you, a woman can take his place just as well. If you ever need anything," she added even more softly, "this is my contact information. Anything at all. And," she paused, "hopefully you won't find it necessary to say thank you then."

"I understand," said Monika, starting to move backwards toward the door.

What in hell was this all about? I don't get out enough. I don't understand anything anymore.

Later, in the car, the boys immediately asked if they were having pizza and fries for dinner. Monika just shook her head. The elder one said: "But even Daddy—" and fell silent, as if he didn't even believe it himself. She changed lanes nervously, although the traffic flowed evenly in all lanes, the rush hour was over, and when she finally hit a welcome red light she turned to the younger boy.

"The teacher said you drew nothing but Angels of Vengeance all day. Is that true?"

The boy nodded.

"I did, but she didn't like it. So then I drew her a baby Godzilla and she was happy."

"Aha. So she said. What about you? Were you sad?"

"I was happy too. She doesn't know that an Angel of Vengeance can change into anything he likes, also a baby Godzilla, and still have the power to destroy." The little boy giggled.

Not only can he speak like an adult, he's just as pleased with his own cleverness as an adult. This went fast.

"Aha. Good on him."

The little boy grew pensive.

"No, not really."

"Why not?"

The boy leaned forward as far as the safety belt would allow and whispered in confidence:

"Because the Angel of Vengeance would like to get rid of his destructive power. But he can't. It's stronger than him."

"You don't know anything," the elder boy cut in. "He can too, he can get rid of it."

The little one looked at him in surprise.

"How?"

"Easy. By destroying everything. Himself too."

Easy. By—

There was a knock on her window.

"What is it?" Monika asked through the narrowest crack she could open with the button. In the rare moments they spent together drinking coffee her assistant would regularly update her on all the horrors happening in the city. Among them were always a few attacks on slow-driving vehicles.

"Excuse me, ma'am, I know, a woman at the wheel and all that, right? But look, the green light's gone. I tried honking, flashing my lights, nothing worked. So I came to ask if I could pay you to drive off. That usually works, don't it, you have to pay and things happen as they're suppose to. What's your usual charge?"

"Charge for what?" asked Monika, bewildered.

"Well, basically, what I had in mind was for you to drive off, right? But if you charge for other stuff too, we could work something out, be glad to. After the kids go to bed, right? Or, maybe, so we shouldn't complicate matters, just drive off when the light turns green again, right? You'll have plenty of time to talk to your kids at home, right? You can do that, can't you? And thanks for understanding."

"Thank you," murmured Monika, closing her window and staring at the traffic lights.

Easy. By destroying everything. Himself too.

At home, despite their loud protests, she cooked the kids some of the natural vegetables Borut had acquired through his channels, adding some regular, non-organic spaghetti as a peace offering. She was running out of everything, *everything*. Or maybe she just didn't know the right combinations. Some of the things in the pantry had no instructions on them. What could they possibly be? Little green globules, little red globules, some sort of spongy things, some strings, piles of paraphernalia for Borut's culinary magic, and far too few boxes you could pop in the microwave for a few minutes. She'd have to go shopping. Tomorrow. She can't take anything anymore today. Today she'd only like to have a glass of wine—

—from one of those bottles I poured down the drain—

She packed the kids off to their room early. She refused to listen to their yells about space butchers, Angels of Vengeance, raging mutants, then cowboys and Indians, capitalists and proletarians, lions and gladiators, and in the end rainbow elephants and lost fawns. Nothing. Nothing. Off to bed. Maybe tomorrow.

"Tomorrow," she announced resolutely, "we go shopping."

"We'd prefer not to go shopping, Mommy. We went with Daddy the last time. In preschool they said shopping was fun. It wasn't fun at all. He didn't buy us anything."

Borut would leave the kids at home when he went shopping. *It's better this way*, he'd say. Monika would object: But Borut! They need to learn! Shopping is life! How are they going to get by in life if they don't know that they have to check the price per pound or quart of products with various types of packaging, not the price of the box? Sometimes you get very little in a big box, and if you don't learn to expect that, it leads to disappointment. And how will they learn what the different colored price tags mean? Discount, on sale, bonus, coupon, just before the expiration date, two for one. The kids need to learn all that or—

Borut would nod. *They'll learn all right*. But he wouldn't take them shopping.

"Daddy didn't, but I will."

You're buying them. We can all be bought, obviously that's another thing you want to teach them.

"Thank you, Mommy!" the little ones cried sycophantically. "Can we stay up a little longer now?"

"I already told you no."

"For sure. But that was before we agreed to go shopping."

Good negotiators. How would Borut convince them? I transfer professionals from one company to another, from one continent to another, and I can't put my own children to bed.

Borut. Borut again.

Admit it: you haven't erased him. You miss him. Admit it. It'll be easier.

She tucked them in and closed the door, not listening to what it was they were offering for overtime.

Don't admit it. Forget. Forget.

In the bathroom: Her face in the mirror. Serious. Tired. Wrinkles around her eyes.

Forget. Forget.

How? Everything's full of him. I feel him even when I brush my teeth. He came up with the brand name for the toothpaste, DissiDent. Forget?

There was no other way. She checked to see if the children were sleeping. They were. She booted her screen.

Don't look at the mail. Nothing matters. He hasn't been in touch.

She didn't look. She logged on to some live security webcams. They were scattered all over town. You could watch if you knew the code. When the Constitutional Court stopped convening over a dispute between the right to privacy and the right to security, security firms pounced on the market niche. They sold access. Regular rate, monthly subscription, hourly rate. The prices depended on locations. Public restrooms were more expensive than intersections. Monika had directed the flow of much of the human resources in security firms, as well as out of them, quite a few people turned out to be too dangerous for security. She demanded that the codes be included in compensation settlements. You never knew when something would come in handy. And you had to keep your finger on the pulse of the street in her line of business. And she herself never went out into the streets.

She watched one camera after another. Old men shooting uppers in side streets thinking no one could see them. Teenage girls stuffing clothes into their bags in changing rooms. A red dot flashed under the footage. Depending on their and their parents' status, the footage would be handed over in out-of-court settlements, sold to the tabloids for general enjoyment, or added to their police records. School children going through their peers' school bags left at the edge of schoolyards, stealing game consoles, switchblades, electric shockers, whatever they could find and sell. The secret life of a peaceful town. Which was no longer secret or peaceful if you had an access code.

Borut was nowhere to be seen.

If he left a message anywhere, he left it here. No more accessing leaking addresses, free-access networks. Here, at home, behind a secure firewall.

There was no other way. She let the mail pour in on her screen.

The usual load of useless junk, the avalanche of spam she'd peruse with interest only days ago. Not that she needed any of the things they recommended, suggested, offered, forwarded. No. She didn't need them. But the commercial messages showed her the pulsating of the world. What was on its way in, what was on its way out. The pulsating she could adjust her trends to.

But none of this mattered now. Neither did her assistant's elated message that the company was doing just fine and that she had *herself* seen to all the important matters that day. It didn't matter to her. Of course it mattered to the assistant. Monika knew: One day the assistant would realize that the *we're all replaceable* slogan, which Monika so loved to repeat, applied to her as well. Maybe she'd realized it today. But it didn't matter.

It didn't matter. Any of it.

Except one thing.

A new message from Borut.

Monika. It seems like a long time. Because so much has happened. So much that I have to get in touch. And because it'll help you if I get in touch. Because you need help. Think about it. I know that you're having problems.

How the hell would you know? We haven't spoken in months! Well, of course you know—*you* are the problem.

You've closed yourself off. You don't open up to anyone so they don't rob you. You have two options. Think. The first one: Stay closed. You've replaced so many people. You could replace anyone they told you to replace. Replace me. The sooner the better. You need someone. You can't function on your own. You're not enough on your own. Find someone. You can always find someone you'll believe loves you.

Idiot. I don't want someone. I want you.

You know that the thing we had was love. The kind of love that was possible. I never really understood why you wanted to be happy. Happy in love? Is it normal? Is it serious? Is it practical? What does the world get from two people who can't see it?

And we didn't see it. We did, but not what it was like. Even more: We did our bit to make it the way it is. Wrong. We were part of the system.

Part of the system? Oh, Borut. *That's the whole point*, being part of the system.

This is the first option. But there's another one. Change. Get out of it. Don't go on replacing people. Because it's wrong. Let people be what they are.

Think about it.

I'll be all right. I hope you'll be all right too.

Borut. You shouldn't have left the company. You're good with words. Your own words. Other people's words. Other people's words become your own, and yours become theirs, they adopt them for their own. Who'll pay you more for what you can do? Who'd pay you for letting people be themselves?

Her reply began to take shape by itself.

Borut. Today I nearly lost it in preschool. I thought something had happened to the boys. I ached all over until the little one came running. Why did you do this to me?

Borut. To love means to stay when every cell in your body is screaming: Run!

Borut. Everybody goes through a midlife crisis. We know about men at the edge of the abyss. And women too. Everyone deals with it the best they can, but most in a less complicated fashion than you. We know that. There are other ways. You could've gone traveling again, for yourself, not for work, you haven't done that in a long time and you used to do it all the time before. You could've bought an unusual car. You could have thrown yourself into the New Age thing. They say it's pleasant. You need to hurry. Osho's long dead, but his place is still clean, they still give everyone an AIDS test at the door. And then there are also others, you should hurry, most prophets die before their time. You could have found yourself a lover. There are enough young girls at your company if you don't have time to go out. You could do it, they'd be discreet, they know it's part of the job. Oh, right, there were, you're no longer working for the company.

Where are you anyway, Borut? Where do you belong? You threw away everything and left. You left the company, you left us. Borut. That's no way to check out. Everyone's replaceable in a company. Me too. You know that. I make my living by replacing them. But in a family, checking out means bankruptcy. I no longer know what the kids are doing. I wander around town with unknown men. Oh, right, and I sleep with them too. And I don't feel guilty. Because you checked out. Left a hole. When they're sinking, people grab onto anything they can. Borut, you who used to always make flawless arrangements. Where did you go wrong? Tell me, Borut.

Goodbye.

She knew what she had to do. *Don't read it. Send it now. If you read it, you'll think about it. And you'll change your mind. You'll want to write it differently. Admit that you're hurting. And then you'll hurt even worse.*

She didn't reread it. She sent it straight away.

Of course it came straight back. *The addressee is currently unavailable. Please try—*

This won't work, Borut. We can't talk like this. I don't understand you.

9.
Tied Twist

"This won't work, Borut. We can't talk like this. I don't understand you."

Maya leaned forward, resting her elbows on the little table and her chin in her palms, and fixed him with her eyes. Steam was slowly rising from their cups. The tearoom was almost empty. Those who had money had to be elsewhere, wherever it was that they made their money. Those who didn't have money couldn't afford to come here. Tea without a napalm aftertaste was getting more and more expensive each year. The tea industry and the narco mafia waged war over every plot of fertile land.

"I mean, you're the one who called *me*. You're the one who said you needed money. I know what you can do. You know what you can do. No problem there. I have work for you, you do it, I pay you, you're happy, I'm happy. Everything hunky-dory. But now you want to do something 'completely different'? And you don't know what? I mean, don't you find that, well, weird? How do you even know if you *can* do something 'completely different'? And how am *I* supposed to know?"

This doesn't look good.

Borut had to admit to himself that he was sorry he hadn't deleted Maya's contact, as he'd told himself to many times. Not that deleting it would have prevented this meeting today. He needed money and Maya was still—
—the first person he called. Besides, everyone in the business of selling words knew how to reach Maya. A symbolic deletion

would have been meaningless. And what had been meaningful was removed a long time ago.

I must have sunken very low to call her after all these years.

"Thanks for coming, Maya. You could've refused. I know how busy you are."

She dismissed it with a wave of her hand and the wisps of steam scattered. Their waiter immediately stepped closer, a dark-skinned man with a long neck. *A Nuba, if I remember the pictures in the World Hunger Atlas correctly.* The tearoom owners tried to be special in every possible way. The skin color of their employ-ees changed in keeping with the changes in global racial trends.

She made another dismissive gesture and the waiter backed away like a wave.

He's learned to move like floating debris. The wages must be high here. Maybe I should start serving tea. Maybe it's already the turn of white heterosexual males to become the endangered species that attracts business.

"You know I would, Borut. For you, always. Whatever the reason, not just business."

You're good, Maya, you're good at this. No wonder your business is doing so well.

"Let's go back to square one. You say there have been some changes in your life. What's changed?"

Changed? Nothing. A short while ago I was living at home and retreated to the hovel I was renting in the Easterners' sector only every now and then. A few months back I was the best-paid creative mind of the Central World. I had enough money in a secret account to live on for two years. I've given it all away over these past couple of months. All I have left now is just enough to pay for this tea, maybe, and that's hoping you pay for your own tea. Even last week I would play with my children every day. Today I sink sickles into people's knees. Changed?

"I don't know if you know about my work situation, I mean, of late. In a nutshell, I no longer work for the Chairman. I had a nest egg, but I've already—let's say, misinvested it."

"Sure I've heard. I know and I get it. And kudos to you. Not many in our line of work have walked out on the Chairman. Almost everyone goes in the other direction, they want to work *for* him. Nobody quits on him. Not until the Chairman does so on their behalf. But the Chairman's one thing, and advertising another, even if few ever dare to think so. What's your beef with advertising? Why this 'something different'? This is what I don't understand. Advertising has given you everything you have."

"That's just it. It's the reason why I'm at this point now."

"What point—sick and tired? I hear you. And believe it or not, also the Chairman could understand. You used to love traveling, you could go somewhere again. No need to burn your bridges, there are other ways. Go talk to him, eat a little humble pie, ask for some time off, go visit some remote corner of the world, there must be a few left, they can't be making all those documentaries in studios, that would be too expensive what with all those big rivers and things. He gives you time off, which is good for him because he doesn't have to pay you, you come back fresh, which is good for you, fresh ideas, he sells them well, good for him, good for you. You're happy, he's happy. Ideal. Trust me, it's been done before."

I come back energized, new victories at work, new guilt trips, new ways of trying to redeem myself.

"Maya, this work, I've really—"

If I say really *had enough of it,* it won't be enough.

"It's one thing to walk out on the Chairman, but to drop out of advertising, that's an entirely different matter. It's not a job, it's a calling! We need commercial advertising! People need help! How can a person decide otherwise, without ads? Everything's getting more and more the same."

Borut smiled. The tea was having a mollifying effect on him. Suddenly he was no longer thinking about his children, as he otherwise was at every moment, but of that cup of tea in that hotel in Darjeeling, that exorbitantly expensive, luxurious hotel where he'd paid a hundred dollars for one night with a light heart, the hundred dollars that were meant for another two weeks of travel, the dollar still had value in those days. He paid and thought: Tonight is a night that anything can happen.

That's also what she said in the morning: This night was a night that anything could happen.

"Everything's becoming more and more the same, except us,

we're becoming less and less equal. But from your office—"

Maya flicked his hand.

"Stop moralizing, please, there are jobs where people can moralize and get paid for it, but not you. It's normal in our line of work to spend so much time convincing other people about how good we are that we end up believing it ourselves. And believing that what we're doing is good. And we have to get paid well for doing good, or no one will believe it's good. That's the way it goes."

If I've gone so far back as to remember that tea, let's go on.

"You know there are quite a few criminals in our business."

"Don't exaggerate, Borut. Okay, the Chairman, him yes, him and his team, but they're not in our business, they're above it, exploiting us, paying us little and selling us dearly, that in itself makes them criminals—"

"Never mind the union catchphrases. Those days are over. I'm talking about something else."

He looked at her.

Her eyes, fixed on the smooth surface of the tea and then swirling up to the ceiling. You can't blame the tiger for eating the antelope. *Now explain to another tiger that an antelope is a living, sentient being. Picture this: You're an antelope running from a tiger, your strength is failing, but you run, you run, the tiger is gaining on you, you think you should've run in the other direction, but it's too late now, the tiger is coming from that direction. And when your legs buckle and the tiger finally catches up, as is bound to happen, you, the antelope say to the tiger: 'You're not going to eat me, are you? Meat is murder. Your steak had feelings once.' And the tiger stops. Thinks. The power of words.*

"Then tell it to me again. I'm not sure I understand you."

"We're changing the world with what we do, Maya. I mean, we as humanity. You know. The butterfly effect and that."

Maya laughed out loud. The only other guest in the tearoom lifted his head in his remote corner.

"I see you're not immune to advertising propaganda yourself. Everyone counts, etcetera, etcetera. It sounds good, being more than just a consumer, doesn't it?"

Borut waited for her to get over her bout of laughter. He continued more softly. The man in the corner went back to staring into his lap. "No, seriously. We're all changing things. Some more, others less, there's no other way. We as creatives, though, change much more because our actions are more visible. And sometimes we do damage even when we think we're doing good. Take, for example, the guy who invented bottled water—he's a criminal. He didn't kill anyone, but because of him we're buying water because we *can* buy it, while natural drinking water deteriorated because it no longer needed to be protected. Nobody drinks it anymore."

"Some people drink it. I'm sure they do in India. Like that time we were there. And drank bottled water."

That's true. And when the taste of that tea wore off I went to ask if it had been made with bottled water. I never got a reply, just long stares and then someone said: "Did you like the tea, sir? And your lady, did she like it? Can we get you anything else?"

"You're right. They still drink it. And in other places as well. And they still have much higher mortality rates than we do. What about you? Do you drink tap water?"

"You know perfectly well nobody normal does that."

"Do you cook with it?"

"You know I don't cook, Borut."

"Water your plants?"

"I don't have any plants."

"Wash your hands? Have you ever wondered why you still have a faucet?"

"Let's stop with these digressions. I told you you're exaggerating. You can also buy spring water if you like. Okay, it's significantly more expensive, but what can you do, the glaciers are melting."

"You understand what I mean, Maya. We're old enough to remember what it was like before. And now we wash with processed water, we put flowers in water we pour from a bottle. Or take paper tissues. Our parents had no problem blowing their noses in cotton handkerchiefs and washing them. Do you ever think about trees?"

Maya was shaking her head.

"Paper tissues are more practical."

"Sure, trees are not practical."

"Disposable is also healthier. More hygienic, you know. The human lifespan is getting longer!"

"Human yes, arboreal no."

"I think you've taken this eco-nonsense way too far. Okay, I'm all for everything natural, but if it goes on like this, the radicals will put a ban on the exploitation of animals by man and also milk and cheese will be gone, not only steaks. The cow doesn't enjoy it one bit, giving milk! And then we'll be only too happy to have synthetic products. If that happens, if they win in court— Aren't you worried about what you're going to eat?"

"I'm worried about what I'm eating now."

It's lucky I hardly eat anything. One thing less to worry about.

"Borut, synthetic food is exactly the same. Only its origin is different. And everything else too. Is exactly the same, I mean. I'm being serious—don't think about the rights of others too much. It hurts your own rights."

"Do you remember my synth food campaign, Maya?"

She gave him an admiring look.

"Do I! Stellar job. Textbook. And I mean that also quite literally. I teach a course in copywriting back at our old alma mater, and guess what examples I give them? Okay, also those old ones: *I like skimmed milk*, and *Europe my country*, and *Vote for the old, they've already eaten*, and *Enough for you*, and *Just do it*, and *The real thing*, but that's history. The present, Borut, was written by you."

"Yes. And because of what I wrote people are losing."

"Losing what? Synth food is the biggest business—"

"Teeth. Hair. Healthy complexions."

"What do you mean?"

"I mean that I walk the streets. And I see people. They stagger. Their skin is not elastic. I look at their teeth. Decayed. I ask them what they eat. Apples, fruit, vegetables? Sure. From the market? They give me weird looks. No way. Isn't that just for the tourists? An apple there costs as much as a computer! We eat what

Synthesis produces, what else. We know what they say: *Better than natural. Longer life.* That's what we eat. And it's cheaper."

Yes, and then their teeth and hair fall out and they can't afford regeneration. And then I give them money, telling them to go get regeneration. And buy real fruit. And real vegetables. And whatever the doctor says. But maybe Synthesis is already taking doctors to seminars on exotic casino islands, the trips are all inclusive, the winnings tax exempt, telling them what to say if their patients no longer want a life better than natural.

"Oh, come on, Borut, what century are you living in? Teeth don't decay only because people don't eat natural fruit. And besides, you know perfectly well people decide for themselves what to invest in, since all health care has to be paid. There are plenty of teeth, but only two kidneys, one heart, and one liver, and they're hard to replace. It's math, pure and simple. You can manage without teeth, it's harder to live without kidneys. It can't all be your fault! Being healthy is simply too expensive, that's just the way it is. They can go live somewhere cheaper."

If they don't have bread, let them eat cake. If you can't afford to get surgery in Switzerland, go to Vietnam. If you can't afford the trip, die at home. Which is the fervent wish of all who have left.

"Of course it's my fault, I'm to blame even according to the Code. I've used words intended to mislead. Longer life didn't mean *their* lives would be longer, it referred to synthetic fruit and vegetables lasting longer because plastic doesn't rot!"

"We both took Econ 101 in our freshman year. I copied from you at the exams, remember? It's cheaper to produce synthetic. That's the main point."

"Yes. That's why all the fruit and vegetables are produced by Synthesis and Synthesis alone. Because it's driven everyone else out of business. Oh, right, except those few individuals who are monitored by the Tourist Association and produce a handful of apples and peaches a year."

"Freshman year economics again. It's only natural for the companies to keep the formulas developed in their labs to themselves; otherwise the Third World would take over production. Just imagine, bananas from South America cheaper than the ones produced in our home labs, despite shipping! Or mangos from Africa? Or pineapples from Asia? Can you imagine that?"

"Yes, actually I can, I can imagine it very easily indeed. And it makes my mouth water. Because thinking of a Synthesis banana makes me nauseous!"

Maya moved her chair closer.

"Borut, you're yelling."

So I am. I can be heard loud and clear. That guy in the dark corner pretending to be drinking tea is already whispering in his sleeve. Maybe I should step over to him and ask: Are you on the Synthesis payroll or the national budget? Or are they already the same?

Maya's voice dropped, becoming raspy, trying to find new paths leading to places it couldn't reach before.

"Listen to me, Borut. You're crazy. I mean, I've always thought you were a bit nuts, but now I know. Don't get me wrong, I don't mind crazy, on the contrary. It kind of suits you. But trying to take the blame on yourself? And if there is no blame to take, you'll make it up? What do you want to be, the next Christ? That's not very original, there are plenty like that around."

Yeah. Sometimes one does make things up. Like closeness over a cup of tea. There are moments like that, sometimes. Sometimes anything seems possible. What if she snuggled so close only because she was afraid of thunder? The fireplace crackling, the roll of thunder in the distance. The monsoon rains were coming, roads might be washed away, it was imperative to go down into the valley quickly. Too much water, all at once.

"Look at it from the other side. That great poster of yours with the large bloodstained sickle. And the slogan. *Don't harm nature. There's another way.* Pure genius. One eats synthetic wheat and is free of guilt. And it tastes the same. Phenomenal. You helped the world. Two bad feelings, hunger and guilt, eliminated in a single stroke."

Phenomenal elimination. In the end, everything is eliminated.

"There's no need to boost my ego, Maya."

My bank balance could use a boost, though.

"Just come out with it, give it to me straight, the business you have in mind. I'm listening."

Maya giggled and motioned to the waiter. "Two more of the same, please," she said.

I hope she picks up the check. I certainly cannot afford another tea at this price.

She took a deep breath and started talking. *Even more softly. For your ears only.*

"I've launched another parallel world. Yeah, I know there are quite a few out there already, but this one's pretty interesting I think. The graphics, the systems, the technostructure, it all works. I have the payment system arranged, the subscriber bases, advertising's never a problem for me, as you know, I'll have to keep product placement in check so it doesn't get too annoying. But I need someone to create the identities. To write the messages for this world."

"Messages about what? The new things offered by this world?"

"Borut! You know where the interest lies. You know perfectly well what it is, that one thing people need but can't buy on the free market."

She giggled again.

"Love, Borut. Tell people what they want to hear. Tell them everything they've always wanted to hear about love but just couldn't find the right TV channel."

"Easy there, Maya. Love—the market's replete with love. Everything's about love. Films, soaps, novels, songs, music, dance . . . It's even used to sell food and washing powder. *Wash with Lance for a blissful romance, Food prepared with love* and that kind of nonsense—"

Maya put her hand over his. An odd, oddly unfamiliar sensation.

"Yes, all right. But that's other people's love. And when people realize that, it makes them sad. If it's unhappy love, they're unhappy too because they're watching unhappy love. And if it's happy it again makes them unhappy because it's so different from what they have. But we'll make and offer them new love. Their own. Custom-made. Well, not just one, obviously, they'll be able to choose from a few. They'll all cost the same, so that won't be a problem, even songs say we're all equal in love. And then communication starts. The entry-entry system. You know."

Their tea arrived, another squirt of a milky trace, a few grains of the white powder, the clinking of cups. Borut could feel his thoughts turning to vapor.

"Two people enter, one at each side of the communication. Naturally, we'll make preference profiles. At the very least we need to know their sexual orientation, right? Well, we'll give them a love affair that matches their preferences. To be clear—you'll be writing for both sides of the affair. Not individually, don't freak out! This'll be a huge business, a whole army of operators couldn't produce enough individual products. No, we'll have stock text chunks with variables that mesh automatically, error-free, and we'll also have proofreaders reading samples and learning, so that you, Borut, can in due time grow tired of the work. See, I've even factored in you getting tired of it!"

Maya clapped her hands enthusiastically. Borut motioned to her to look at the other guest in the tearoom, who was again talking to his sleeve, and she immediately dropped her voice.

"There have been systems like this before, for sure, but they had one major flaw. Live contact. The system simply cannot allow that. As long as the communication follows the templates, the customers are happy. The templates have been tested, there's no possibility of conflict, only lovey-dovey on both sides. Everyone can be sexier and smarter over the computer than they really are—but to remain that way they have to stay there. If you move on to live contact, things get different. There are conflicts straight away; the preference profiles are not precise enough, obviously. And if there is no conflict, if they're both happy, they no longer need a parallel world, the real one's good enough for them and we've lost them. That's why live contact will be made impossible, everything will be coded ad infinitum. Not even you and me could get at our real identities. The web is the final frontier of identity."

"A site with feelings?"

"A site with feelings."

"That's an awesome scheme, Maya."

Maya's look softened.

"Sure it is. I told you so. I'm so glad you agree with my view."

"It could be a slam dunk. There's one tiny problem. It doesn't really surprise me, though, that you haven't thought of it."

Borut bit his tongue. Ever since he started changing phrases into reality he felt better, considerably better. Now the salty taste of his blood brought him the soothing message: *You're alive. You're still alive. It could also be different. You thought about it a lot, about how it could be different, about how it should be different. But it isn't, you're alive and you feel pain. And you're changing what is wrong.*

"Tell me."

"There's no real interface for emotions yet. Emotions have to be genuine."

Maya pressed her lips together and Borut watched, enchanted, as swollen capillaries became visible through the layers of lipstick. *You're still alive too. You pretend to have become digitized, but you're not. When you get upset, you press your lips together. If I bit you, you'd bleed. And, if I remember correctly, enjoy it too.*

"Come on, really? Genuine? Online *is* genuine. More genuine than anywhere else! Everything's moved online. Everything. Except for emotions. Everything else is there. Shopping, information, sex, opinions, revolutions. As soon as someone loses a job, they voice their opinions on forums and talk about everything—what's wrong, how it should be done. They're on all the forums. Genuine? What's fake about a genuine choice from among created templates? This is the kind of freedom we want, Borut. We fall for certain types, some women for photographers, some men for women physicians, others for humanitarian workers, or mountain climbers."

"The choice may be genuine. But the chosen emotions are not."

Maya was shaking her head.

"Life's too short for that much choosing! We're being offered certain types at every instant. The mass media is full of typology-based advice: The kind of gift to choose for your parents, your kids, your husband, your lover. Why is it that in every supermarket the yogurt is next to the milk rather than next to the cleaning products? You could put those fridges anywhere. And candy next to cookies? All chain stores boast they are different, and about their comparative advantages—how come none of them reverse the display? Because the buyers would have a hard time finding their way around! People don't want the same, but they want the same possibility to choose."

"You're not going to believe this, Maya, but the Chairman and I just talked about this same thing a very short while ago."

Borut held his breath to see what she would say. Something along the lines of *you must be the last person who saw him alive then* could follow. But no, she pursued her lips and started talking, her words cutting like a knife.

"If the Chairman is still on speaking terms with you, I don't know what we're doing here at all. Just tell him you want your job back, what are you waiting for? I'll never be able to throw the kind of money your way he can. And you know yourself that he pays the people he speaks to a lot. Especially since there aren't that many left."

You're offended. I haven't been blown away by your grand design. I know you. I still know you. We haven't been apart long enough.

She placed her hand over his.

"He's lonely."

You should know.

Borut was horrified to feel the bile rising in him. *You're the one who comforted him in his hours of loneliness, that's why your little agency still exists.*

He immediately took the sting out of his thoughts.

Not like this. Not with her. She went through a rough patch because of me. I'll have to do it differently.

"Look, Maya, I'm not the right guy for this. I don't have the right kind of experience. You know me, when it comes to love—"

Maya sighed.

"Oh, come on, who is the right guy then? I've tried all sorts. I've had copywriters who said they were the best in the business. They came up with identities of horny nurses, golfing chief surgeons, corporate lawyers who'd divvied up among themselves the ownership of all of the city's brothels and casinos, overworked single moms having meaningless sex with insensitive men who'd come for a beer to the bar where they work the nightshift. I told them nobody wanted this kind of thing and they'd bring me site traffic and ranking diagrams and tell me it was a perfect mix. What am I going to do with guys like that? Then I had rock stars. What good does it do me if at concerts teenage girls cuff themselves to the stars' ankles if they come too close to the edge of the stage? What good does it do them? Have you ever tried to get it on with a teenager who's handcuffed to your ankle? You haven't? Just try it, you'll see, it's not easy. Nothing but expenses. You have no idea what kind of damages parents sue for when they find their cherished baby-girl cuffed to a shadowy guy like this. He's even expected to pay for the spoons missing from the school cafeteria and found in some dark corner, scorched on the bottom. And that means I have to pay, because he's on my payroll! No more wild boys. That's not what I pictured, Borut. I pictured myself standing on the stage, leaning on the mike stand, my hair streaming in the wind, fog enveloping my feet, beefy young guys playing electric guitars behind me, while I groan into the mike *Where have all the good men gone, and where are all the gods? I need a hero, and he's gotta be larger than life.* And then one just like that leaps onto the stage, shoves the security guys out of the way, throws me over his shoulder and carries me off somewhere, I don't know, to some fusty basement apartment for all I care, and doesn't let me out for five days, until we've tried every position we've ever seen in any porn movie and then maybe invent a few more of our own. That, Borut. Why isn't that on the market yet?"

"Come on, you're blowing it out of proportion. There are good men out there."

Maya carefully put down her cup, from which the precious tea had been splashing around during her recital, pulled her chair closer, and whispered:

"Is that so? Well, if you find me one, I'll pay you straight up. No need to write anything. What about your missus, doesn't she have a human resource management firm? Maybe she can give you a hand with this. I'd like to have one such good resource diverted directly to me now, please."

Borut shook his head in disbelief.

"Oh, please. Look at yourself, Maya, you look great, you're fun, anyone would be happy to have you. You should just look around a little and you'll be fine. You haven't tried hard enough."

"I have looked around. You think I haven't looked around, Borut? You really think I'd first come asking you, really? I mean I've spent all night online countless times. All those hot dating sites, enough to drive you crazy. Just typologies. Women dumped by their husbands for younger lovers, and men dumped by their wives who took everything, including the children. And then the flames of the war between the sexes lick the keyboard. The things you don't get! Things have changed really drastically. The price of porn and snuff movies, footage of actual deaths used to be pretty steep. Now people put it online themselves. But what kind of stuff! Not only is it badly shot technically, it's also lousy in terms of *content.* When some dictator is hanged and the footage is released, everybody hangs themselves the same way for months. And when some starlet makes an ostensible home movie of jumping some guy's bones, all the teenage girls will only do her positions! And the starlet had just been repeating the script of some porn flick herself! You can't sublimate ads into things like that, you'd have to *pay* people to watch.

"So, first I watched, waited, and was disgusted. Then I realized I'd have to put myself on view and up for selection. I had the best pro take my pictures, blurring my face, of course, and with a few tactical retouches, I tell you, really good, I got turned on myself, although you know women leave me cold. For the time being, I'll say, for the time being, because the situation with men doesn't look too good. In short, I put myself out there. Offers just poured in, like I was giving away power company stocks. Believe me, so much was going on I couldn't keep up. There were photos galore, and what photos. Lots of guys cradling guns. Others with dogs foaming at the mouth, straining against their leashes. Does a thing like that turn you on? Apparently it does some people. Why else would you post that on a dating site? I also got responses from women, showing their flabby crotches to the camera despite the fact that I'd specifically stated I was looking for a man, a man, just one single guy. Well, I can't blame the poor women, I did look hot in those photos, a real pro took them, I tell you.

"In short, nothing. Well, I said to myself, if we've come this far, let's push it a bit further. And I replied to a few invites. Now that was a disaster. Do you think it's enjoyable not to know which stranger is going to ruin your weekend by displaying his ego issues, demanding you buy parachuting gear because you have to do things together, and then end up by showing you his room at his parents' place, including his collection of teddy bears? So boring! And when you don't know and bet yourself how long some guy is going to take to call and ask you for a drink and then nothing happens over that drink and you don't hear from him again for another five months.

"I've been for lunch with a walk afterwards, and the man spent the entire two hours telecommunicating. I ate my meal in peace and then I sat on a parapet for a while, waiting to see if it would end. And he asked me if there was anything the matter. I said, well, this is one of my bad dates. And he says—but this isn't a date. Right, what is it then—a meeting of the chamber of commerce? And then he spent the rest of the time literally crying over the millions he had lost on his last date because his battery went dead and he couldn't find a charger anywhere. I never saw him again. Let him charge it with someone else."

Borut shook his head.

"I can't believe what you're saying."

"Better believe it, because I really don't want to go over this story again to make it sound more convincing. Here's the net balance, to recap: A couple of good photos, hundreds of hours lost, no orgasms, not to mention no guy that one would want to see more than once. And you tell me I haven't tried hard enough. Thank you for understanding."

"This parallel world of yours—you'd be the first one to use it, wouldn't you?"

"Sure I would! Haven't I been telling you for the last ten minutes that I'm the ideal target group? I would, on one condition. If you wrote it. But you won't, will you?"

"No, Maya, I won't. It's not my thing. Emotions instead of another—"

My own emotions are weird enough.

"I could feel it, Borut. In that case we won't, will we. Too bad. I'm sorry. Can I tell you something now that we're not going to be partners? This guilt of yours. The way you're constantly trying to take the blame for something. I understand, there are people who simply *want* the blame. And if no other way, they make something up. You're one of them. You know. You know why we split up."

He looked at the ground. His nose filled with the scent of dry branches crackling in the hotel fireplace and the hundred-year-old silk rug they had lain on.

"I don't want to go into that now—"

"Don't say you don't want to go into that *now*, you never want to go into that, or never have. You preferred to do it the way you did, so that we split up and you could be to blame, better that than talk about it. And you know something? It doesn't make sense that I was the one who had to comfort you. And that I still do. It's usually the other way around."

"I know what I did was wrong."

"Don't bother, I won't be nice and let you take the blame, you don't deserve it. Why do you keep trying so hard to take the blame? Borut, it *had* to be that way, we *had* to get rid of the baby, we weren't ready, we were too young, we didn't have the strength, we just couldn't. Sure it hurt, and I know it must've hurt you as well. But so what, I can take a little pain, and besides, what else was there to do? Drop out of university, at least one of us, I at least for a while, and go live with that tyrant of your mother who couldn't even stand your father, quit traveling and spend the rest of our lives wondering whether we'd done the right thing, and with the right man. Or the right woman. We just didn't have the strength for that kind of thing back then. That's how it was."

Maya rose to her feet.

"Honestly, Borut—I'm glad for you that you made it. Even if it was with another woman. But you know something?"

"What?"

"You're not wearing your wedding ring anymore."

He nodded.

"It took a long time."

And it did, but what—wearing it or taking it off?

She nodded.

"I know, you don't have it easy either. But still. At least you have children. And a wife of sorts. What do I have? An idea my ex doesn't like," she said. She waved for the waiter, shook her head no to Borut's attempts to scrape up some cash in his pockets, and took out her communicator. *A bill equal to an amount one could live off of in Iran for two months.*

It was no longer raining. A city seen in puddles is nicer than the reality, thought Borut. *Neon blurs, the hard edges soften.*

"You're not working on your perfect mix anymore?"

"I quit mixing. Mashing together stuff that isn't mine. What for? A DJ has no other purpose in life than to pair this with that. There are other things in life."

"You're giving up control again, aren't you? You know, you're very good at pairing things. That's why I thought of you. Don't give up. You're the right person for it. Make your mix. It doesn't matter what you highlight. It's what in the background that matters. The beat matters. There's no breathing without the beat. No work. No love. Even prophets put a beat under their thoughts. There is no other way."

"That's exactly why I quit. The beat that was taking shape was too ordinary. Too *pop.*"

"It has to be pop, or it doesn't penetrate. It stays on the surface. And you're looking for something that'll jolt them, I know you."

She glanced around the street and hugged him.

She checked for the nearest security camera. Hugging a creative who's opted out. Bad for business. I have to hand it to you, Maya, you sure know the ropes.

"You know, Borut, I could sleep with you."

"I know. But you won't."

"Why not? It would make you feel better."

"I know that too. But—"

—but I'd rather remember that night in Darjeeling—
"—but I can't. I'm in love with someone else."
Maya weighed his words.
"Then why aren't you with her?"
"I can't do that either."
"Why not?"
He pondered a long time before replying:
"This I don't know."

Because she builds what I want to tear down?
Because she is the same and I'm different?
Because I don't want her and the kids to be involved when some-
thing happens?

She stepped back, caressed his arm and smiled.
"You know why you were so good at presentations, Borut?
Your demeanor said: This man knows exactly what he's going to
do, and he's going to do it very well. And you know why you
weren't good enough to stop playing with words and become a
presenter? Because no one could ever tell *what* it was that you
were going to do so well. You would sell what you did to the
client in such a way that they were sure they were getting exactly
what they wanted. They just never knew what that was."
The man who had been talking to his sleeve in the corner of
the tearoom walked past them. He was still talking to his sleeve,
caressing it, an expression of pure love on his face; his shirt looked
very expensive. They caught a few words: *Dearest . . . touching my*
body . . . so endlessly soft . . .
Maybe I'm being unjust. Maybe he sold a kidney to buy a
designer shirt.
Borut smiled. The lights changed. Maya proffered her cheek,
He absent-mindedly kissed it and ran across the street. On the
other side he turned to look back. Maya waved. She looked different in the puddle. More melted. More real.
The people passing him were loaded with plastic shopping
bags, some with paper bags. They exuded giddiness. The sales
had started.

10.
Straight-Line Kolo

THE PEOPLE PASSING them were loaded with plastic shopping bags, some with paper bags. They exuded giddiness. The sales had started. Overflowing shopping carts were pushed by Sherpas. The further they went into the sprawl of the shopping malls, the harder it was to make their way through. The jungle of consumption was overgrowing the city. The town planners tried to contain the riotous growth, but a shoot would creep into the urban tissue in one place, then in another, and, in accordance with the equal competition principle, others could then also open up shop in the neighborhood. Then migrations would start. Some residents moved out, others moved in, each following their favorite brands and making sure there was reserved parking. The price of a square foot of living space was rising, although the pace varied depending on the neighborhood. Buying real estate was like Russian roulette. You never knew whether tomorrow you would have a clean new supermarket next door or if the folklore activists would successfully push for a new area to be planted with whatever and then you'd have the smell of natural fertilizers right under your windows.

The boys gawked at the shop windows and pointed out the glitziest items to each other. They spelled out the shiny lettering, competing to see who'd be the first to find words like BEST BARGAINS! TODAY ONLY! and FINAL DAY OF SALE! The logic behind it wasn't quite clear. As soon as the beginning of the sales was announced and the most determined shoppers crawled out of their sleeping bags and made a dash for the objects of their desire, every retail chain followed its own strategy. Some of them ended the sales straight away, figuring, with good reason, that people wouldn't notice anyway, and if they did, they could still say that their goods were the cheapest anyway. Other stores would, when running out of the items most in demand, buy similar merchandise in other, cheaper stores, change the tags, triple the price, and immediately reduce it by half in the sales. People tapped at their communicators, checking if the prices matched the promised slash percentage, nodded, and happily piled things into their carts. Stores hired students to rush about in the crowd, calling out to one another: *Look at this! How cheap! Look! Get one for me too!* Pushing them away, people tried to figure out what new trend the young people had spotted. If the guessing went on for too long, a student would grab a fancy piece of clothing, yelp happily while looking at the price tag, and ostensibly drop the item accidentally, only to pout when someone else snatched it up triumphantly. And if that someone should be so naive as to offer to give her the garment back, saying the rule of first touch applied, she would thank them and say that that was the way the cookie crumbled, you win some, you lose some, and it would be the other way around next time. The buyers would nod; we finally won one this time, they thought, it was about time.

It took forever to get to the groceries. Ever since rest stations with beds at a reasonable hourly rate started being added to malls a person didn't need to go home at all; as long as one's payment routes stayed open, one could spend days on end in total shopping. Temptations lurked at every turn and with enthusiastic cries the boys would call Monika's attention to this or that thing offered almost for free in all manner of stores. She kept shaking her head no, stubbornly refusing to be intimidated by the shocked looks passersby were giving her; obviously they hadn't walked past such a cold-hearted mother in a long time. She got stuck at intersections a few times, unable to decide in which direction to go, and the boys always helped out by pointing which way the cookies they'd been promised lay, until in the end her conscience began to trouble her. They were contributing their share to the family mission, should they perhaps also participate in the choosing? How would Borut have solved this?

Borut would have left the children at home. And had he taken them with him, he would have told them beforehand that they could not choose anything for themselves. Unless they paid for it with their own money, which they were saving up for the entry fee to a pig-of-the-day contest.

Eventually they reached the hypermarket. Looking around her, Monika was perplexed. She hadn't been grocery shopping in a long time. *Could the layout have changed or is everything just so much bigger that I can't find my way around anymore?* She found herself in unfamiliar, unexplored territory. Milk was no longer where it used to be, there were whole aisles of things she had never seen before and she had no idea whether she needed them or not. She enviously watched people speeding by, their hands reaching left and right, their carts filling up. *These are teams equipped to live a happy family life. What about us? What do we actually need? It'll be hard to choose without a shopping list. There's no food at home, that much is certain, but what* are *those things that we combine to make delicious breakfasts and lunches and dinners?* A lot of the food Borut used to bring home had instructions for use on the packaging. Those that didn't he knew about anyway. And if she happened to be cooking and came up against a blank, she could always ask him. If you know the ingredients you're supposed to put in a certain dish—the number of possible combinations is always limited—cooking is no more complicated than solving a Rubik's cube. But here, amidst the endless aisles, the choice was too vast. She found some solace at first in the fact that certain things were too high up anyway and out of her reach, at least she wouldn't have to decide about them. Then she realized with a sinking heart that the shelves reaching to the sky stocked the same things as the shelves below.

There seemed to be no end to the boxes of cookies. People dragged their feet listlessly. Every now and then someone would recognize a familiar brand and immediate block the way to it with their cart, as though the other wanderers might instantly recognize the correct choice and steal everything right from under their noses. Not that it happened; everyone persisted in uncertainty. A woman desperately kept asking her husband: "Which ones do we want?" The man was studying the small print on the packages, reading the quantities of preservatives and stimulants under his breath. "Don't you like any of the packaging?" he replied without looking up. The woman's eyes wandered over the shelves perplexedly. "I don't know," she said. The man didn't reply. He kept picking boxes off the shelves, turning them over, returning them to the shelves.

The fruit was stacked in impeccable symmetry. There must have been some philosophy underpinning the system; certain piles were reminiscent of ancient pyramids, temples of forgotten creeds. A man picked an apple off the stacked heap and inspected it suspiciously, and a few other apples rolled off and onto the floor, bouncing high like tennis balls. The choices were hard to make, the supply was too varied. There were dozens of sorts of apples, and melons in all fashionable nuances. Everything seemed to be in season, the fruit was polished, gleaming, the women looked at their reflections in smooth nectarine skins, fixing their hair. People tore flimsy plastic bags off the rack and tried to figure out on which side they open.

A woman in a checkout line collapsed, upturning a stand with astral charts. The Libras fluttered about the place, the Gemini remained stuck together, animal signs dismally lay on the floor all mixed together in astral bestiality. From a raised cubicle in a remote corner a stocky man appeared, walking tiredly toward her, craning his neck to get a better view. The girl at the cash register said: "Leon, Prozac flour," and he replied while approaching the fallen woman: "Seventy-nine." His chest pocket was crammed full of various scanners.

The boys kept trying to sneak things into the cart. Monika doggedly returned the objects they had chosen for their colorful packaging or pulsing fluorescent barcodes to the shelves. Pills against sclerosis, outboard motor lubricant, pet penguin food. The boys would try to object every now and then, but when Monika asked them what it was that they had actually picked off the shelf, they fell silent and started looking around for the next splash of color. Their attention span was short, flitting from one thing to the next.

In the main aisle people crowded around tasting and recommendation stalls. Popular home shopping network preachers lent their aura to products with substantial promotional budgets. The crowds around them were the thickest; the remaining shoppers gathered around those whose best promoting years were long gone. Monika saw a familiar face among them. She knew them all by sight, one of her office monitors was constantly tuned to home shopping channels, but she had actually spoken to this man in her office a while ago, not only to his face on a screen, but his whole body in the room. He came in despair, looking for a job as a social worker, and she re-specialized him, free of charge, into a loyalty program host, then sold him for big money to a dermatological clinic, where he persuaded people not to contract any other kind of disease. Now he was here. *What's happened to dermatology?* Monika thought she noticed an increasing number of people in the streets who didn't seem to fit into their skins well—couldn't they find professional help? He was breaking up chocolate into pieces and offering it to passing shoppers. They stuffed it into their mouths, some of them reaching into the bin before him and putting a few bars into their carts, while the host nodded encouragingly: *Congratulations, you've made the right choice.*

His mouth spewed his selling mantra, his lips glossy with chocolate.

"Listen up, you non-stop shoppers! Do you yearn for something sweet? Give yourself a Choco-bite treat! Why say no to pleasure? All you need is the right measure! And don't believe those lies¬—that it's unhealthy and your weight will rise! That's not the story of our brand! You can feast on what's in *my* hand! And don't believe that *lovey-dovey's* better, *that* will only stretch your sweater! Dovey will just fly away or make you wait, while Choco-bite's your forever mate!"

He waved his hand over the children clustering around him. They watched to see what their parents would do. Would they take some chocolate from the stand or not? The parents' hands began moving. Smiles of satisfaction settled on the children's faces.

Borut would say—smart. Children are for chocolate anyway. They don't need an extra story. It's the adults you have to sell the story to. It's the adults that pay.

"We're not against it, though." the promoter hurried on.

"Far from that, you know. Increase the birth rate! Let the nation thrive! A fertile state—that's what keeps us alive! Just couple it with Choco-bite for a double sensual delight."

Of course his company would thrive with more people. More people more consumption. We need new people. We all do. Also the morgues want work. And the cemeteries. Even though they're privatized now, business is in a slump. There are fewer and fewer dead people. Because fewer and fewer are born. They have to import corpses if they want to stay in the black.

The man caught sight of Monika. He nodded.

"It's better. Much better," he whispered and motioned for her to step closer.

She stepped closer.

"It's *really* good," he said and placed two large bars in her cart. "Believe me. Here, take this. From me."

"How are you?" asked Monika. *I wanted to say* how did you end up here? *but I couldn't, it's all going too fast—*

The man gave her another amicable nod. "It's better. I'm no longer roping them in. Now I'm inside. Much better," he said, smiled again, and started from the top:

"Listen up, you non-stop shoppers! Do you yearn for something sweet—"

Monika turned to her children only to find that they were no longer by her side.

She looked behind her. A crowd of people. To her left. A crowd. To her right. A crowd. The crowd was pushing her away from the chocolate man, she grabbed on to her cart, pushing it in front of her to ram her way through the masses of people—

The boys. Where have they gone?

She laid her eyes on one of them, pulled him to her, only to realize that he wasn't hers when he turned, that she'd made a mistake. The boy started crying, his mother immediately looming, hissing something indeterminate in her direction and pulling him away.

The boys. Where have they gone?

There were children all over the place. Many resembled hers, same clothes, same hair, similar looking, but none of them waved when she met their eyes, they all averted their gaze, some of them sticking their tongue out first. It was often in the news on television, reports about scary strangers who snatched children right from under their incautious daddies' and mommies' noses, to sell them to unknown ladies for god knows what purposes, it was often in the news, and in their eyes she was obviously becoming one of those evil strangers—

No. It doesn't matter. What matters—

The children were whispering to their parents and pointing at her.

I have now obviously become the incautious mommy.

Monika's head was spinning. She began to lose her grip on the cart handle, so she grasped it until the metal bit into her palms. She thought the chocolate in her cart was sure to be melting by now, just a few more moments and it would start to drip through the mesh and onto the floor, it would make a bubbling puddle there and she'd step into it, slip, break something, people would sidestep to avoid her as long as possible, then they'd step over her, that Leon with the scanners in his chest pocket would look at her in suspicion, *Not another one! What's with this day! What an astral confusion!* And she would just lie there, looking at the merchandise on the bottom shelves nobody reaches for because the manufacturers hadn't paid enough for product placement, useless stuff, and she would hurt, she'd surely break something and she'd be in pain—

A man approached. He stood squarely in front of her and fixed her with his eyes.

"Lady, my son has told me about you."

"About me?"

What's happened to them?

"I think you should leave the store."

"I'm looking for my children," she muttered. "Have you—"

"Not here. Look, I'm not looking for trouble. With the job I have I can't afford to break your nose here with all these cameras around. But I tell you, if I met you in a dark alley—"

"My children—"

"Don't give me that *my children* yarn. I've been around, I

know the world. It's my job. These cameras—I can get the footage, you know. And if ever a child goes missing and you're anywhere near on camera—you know I can find you. It's my job."

I should say something now, I should defend myself, but—

"Help me find my children."

The man reached inside his jacket.

Do they have metal detectors in this store? Not all stores do—

He kept it inside a while, before pulling it out. He held his
communicator in the direction of her face for a moment.

I should lift my hands, but I can't let go of the cart—

There was a click.

"I have your picture. A lot could transpire if anything happens. This was your last warning," he said and turned away.
Monika looked on as a boy the same age as her own hugged
him, then turned to her and stuck his tongue out. They left in
the direction of the cosmetics aisles.

Now they're going to get Mommy. A together family—

She felt a tug on her arm. Hunching her head between her
shoulders, she turned around. It was her sons.

"Are you okay, Mommy?" the elder one sounded worried.

"Let's go home, Mommy," said the younger one. "You don't
look so good."

Monika nodded and the boys led her to the checkout line,
unloaded everything from their cart onto the line, reached inside
her purse for the plastic, showed her which slot to insert it in and
where to press her finger. Monika completely stopped perceiving
things, only feeling a slight wave of humiliation and betrayal
when she saw that she had been charged the regular retail price
for the chocolate.

The woman at the register smiled at her in a friendly fashion:

"Shopping's the thing. In religion, the future is behind us. In
shopping, the present is eternal."

"Excuse me?" said Monika.

"Shopping's the thing. In religion, the future is behind us. In
shopping, the present is eternal."

"I don't understand."

The woman at the register frowned and looked at her feet. She scraped her foot and there came a faint crackling sound.

"Me neither," she said under her breath. "It's our new motto. We're trying it out."

"I see," said Monika. "And you haven't been told what it means?"

"No, we haven't. And we asked. During training. And they told us never mind. And then we went for coffee together during the break, and one of them said that they didn't know either."

The maintenance man came stomping up. Drops of sweat falling off his face splattered on the conveyor belt. The woman grimaced and reached for a paper towel. He didn't notice.

"Your communicator's not working," he said, then, wincing, turned to Monika and said more slowly: "Welcome to our store. I hope you have enjoyed your shopping experience." Dropping to the young woman's feet, he said: "The wire's disconnected. For the second time this week!"

The girl at the register spread her arms.

"Why is it so loose at my station?" she said and winked at Monika.

"I'll fix it," said the maintenance guy. "You'll fix something for me next time, right?" He started inserting the wire back into the circuit.

The girl took his hand. "You know we're not supposed to get entangled with people at work," she told him sweetly and dropped his hand. The big guy looked at the loose end of the wire in his hand and back at her. A red light on his belt started flashing.

"Needs to be fixed, right? Gotta go on, right?"

Nodding sourly, he inserted the wire into some socket and hurried off.

"We are glad of your custom," said the girl in a trained voice and nodded to Monika.

Monika proffered her hand, slipping her business card into her palm.

"Call me when the time comes," she whispered. "Everyone has to change their job sometime."

You can definitely find a better one, no doubt about that. And if you've gone through this charade because you know what I do, all the more.

The children were holding her by the hand, one on each side.

"Don't get lost again, Mommy. Please."

"Sure. Sure—Where's our car?"

"We take a turn at the FINAL DAY OF SALE. Then left at TODAY ONLY and right at BEST BARGAINS. Out the door. To the car park. There you'll know which car is ours. Right?"

They looked at her, concerned.

"Of course I'll know which car is ours," she murmured in desperation.

"Because I don't want to go home with some other car," the younger one said. "Because our car is the best." Then he gave her hand a tug: "Mommy! Is our car also the best bargain? The best and the best bargain?"

"I don't know," said Monika, confused. "Daddy made all the arrangements."

"Oh, right," nodded the little boy. "Right, Daddy made all the arrangements." He paused, like he was puzzling over something. "What about you, Mommy?"

"Me?"

"What do you do?"

"I manage—I manage human resources."

At least I have, until today. And tomorrow? Ask me the day after tomorrow.

"Uh-huh.—What's that?"

"You'll find out when you're bigger."

"Uh-huh." Monika could feel resentment replacing curiosity. "Sorry I asked."

"It's okay. I just—"

"Yes?"

"Everything's okay."

"Mommy? You just—?"

Everything's okay. I just don't know what I'm actually doing.

11.
Tribal Breaking

Everything's okay. I just don't know what I'm actually doing.

"Borut! Hey, Borut, stop pretending you can't hear me!"

The people in the street were turning their heads. In his direction, all of them.

"Borut, you can't be *that* lost in thought, not even you, I know you. How are you?"

"I'm okay, Mom."

"In that case, you're hiding it well. Because you certainly don't look okay. You should get more sleep. You work too hard. And you're pale and you've lost weight. I know that wife of yours doesn't cook, if you're no good at something you're just no good at it, there's no getting around that, but a person should eat at home, you can only really stuff your face out of sight of the public eye! Well, let's go get some lunch."

"You know I don't eat most things. Maybe it'd be better if we just kept going to wherever we were going."

"We're not going to wherever we were going. I'll starve a little with you. Come, I've heard of a new place where they also serve your bird feed. Apparently it's quite trendy now."

The maître d' who tried to steer them at the door didn't stand a chance. Borut's mother indicated the table she wanted and pulled Borut by the sleeve.

"Come, we'll be out of the way a bit over there. More intimate. Please don't hold back. We've come here to eat. You are, of course, also free to tell me anything. How are the kids? Fine?"

I wish I knew.

"Fine. How's Dad?"

She waved it off.

"We're not here to talk about your father. You know there's not much to tell about him. Order anything you like, please."

Perusing the menu, Borut was at a loss. The waiter stepped up helpfully to offer professional assistance. Indicating generally the list of vegetarian dishes, Borut asked: "Sorry, this is my first time here . . . Are these Synthesis vegetables?"

Without changing his expression, the waiter nodded and leaned closer:

"Naturally," he said quietly, "we have another menu for connoisseurs."

The other menu was much thinner, not only because it was bound in artificial fig leaves, unlike the previous one in artificial leather. Many of the dishes bore the same name in both menus, but the prices in this one were several times higher. Borut picked some things whose flavor he had already forgotten, then passed the menu to his mother.

"I'll have the same," she turned to the waiter. "To see what my son eats."

"Excellent choice, madam."

His mother nodded as though she couldn't agree more, waited for the waiter to leave, then said:

"I hear you're no longer with the Chairman."

"Mom, how—"

"Let's level with one another. You know I move in circles where I also learn things I don't even want to know. And if it concerns my people, I listen. What should I do? Pretend I don't care?"

"No, but—"

"You have no job, then. Do you need money? You know I have more than enough. Apparently you can't take it with you when you go. And that's a thing I'll have to start thinking about someday soon."

That's actually true. But—

"Mom, you know I can't take money from you anymore."

His mother took hold of his hand.

A cold touch. Unpleasant.

"Come on, Borut. You're not so old that you really couldn't. And neither am I."

"Mom, I have my own—"

"Children, yes, I know, that's why I'm offering."

"—income, my own savings—"

"There's no shame in getting fired. It happens to everyone." She paused, her eyes boring into him. "You haven't told Monika, have you? I sure hope not. I'll make a confession, Borut: I've never liked that woman."

"I know, Mom. You've never tried to hide it. And besides, you never liked any of the others either."

"There were others? Well, I don't like her. You know how it is. I don't think the times are over yet when men make the decisions and women take care of the children and cook. And that's not exactly the situation with you two, is it? Well, I have a hard time putting up with bossy women. I was actually quite relieved when you stopped coming for lunch on Sundays. Sure, I would've loved to see the little ones every now and then, and I kind of resent only learning about you from business reports, but—"

The waiter approached and she fell silent. Leaning over, he whispered in Borut's ear which of his selections were not available and what they could offer instead. Borut was too upset to pay attention, let alone object. He nodded yes to all the suggestions and the waiter left again.

"I have a solution for you, Borut. You can come work for our company. You know I still have connections from my years in Internal Affairs, and a lot of the operations are still going strong. We never received enough funding, we always had to find other resources. We dealt in cars, then imported oil, then exported plutonium, then organs, this and that. Whatever was going. One had to be flexible. Whatever there was a market for. Nowadays we're into insemination. It's the leading secret internal service. A sperm bank. I suppose you know that most men's semen is defective nowadays. Of course, if women manage to get it the natural way in the first place. That's why it's much smarter to pay a reputable institution, that way you at least know what you're getting. Degeneration, what can I say. You're an exception, of course, look at your children—"

She paused.

She's trying to remember their names.

She scraped her chair closer to his and Borut thought how uncomfortable he had been for the last twenty years whenever his mother sat close enough to touch him.

"Listen, you're not experiencing difficulties with—yet? Because with your father, you know, that happened very early on. It's a good thing I was at least able to squeeze you out of him. But our people can fix that now, we have good stuff, our own labs, lots of connections with specialists in the field. Only the side effects are still a matter of some divided opinion, but nobody lives forever anyway."

He burst into laughter. His mother looked at him in astonishment.

"Borut! Are you all right? I don't think I've said anything particularly funny!"

Always helpful, the waiter brought a small bottle of water. Before setting it down on the table, he checked the use-by date, frowned, took it away, and returned with another one.

"Sorry, Mom, but I never really expected to be offered such a career. An inseminator! And proposed by my own mother!"

"Don't scoff, Borut," said his mother severely. "I'm only trying to help out. Help you and—the nation, or how shall I put it."

Borut shook his head.

"I have enough kids, Mom. Above the national average."

His mother nodded.

"Fine. Understood. If you don't want this, I can put in a good word for you with the Chairman. You know we go back a long time. To our days in Internal Affairs. We've kept in touch."

Borut frowned.

"You have? And have you been in touch lately?"

He can't have vanished without a whisper. Even if he hasn't been shot. It must have reached the media by now! Okay, the public relations office must have deemed that any news would be bad news, the

man at the head of the company must appear to be an unbreakable
tough guy, and the Chairman is the biggest media space buyer, so—
But there are also independent tabloids—

"Not for a while now. Not since—"

A long pause.

This must be a very special moment, mother, you rarely choose
your words.

"—since I asked him for a favor. Which I of course paid back
with another favor. But that was a long time ago."

Embarrassed, Borut glanced around the restaurant. A man
was sitting with a boy at one of the tables in the back, probably a father with his preschooler. They were seated too far away
for Borut to discern whether they'd ordered real or synthetic
vegetables.

Their lunch arrived. His mother eyed the contents of her
plate suspiciously.

"You *eat* this, Borut? These greens look somehow, how shall
I put it, worn—"

"You're old enough, Mom, to remember what vegetables used
to look like. Like this."

"Possibly, but technology has moved on, and if a fresh appearance can be preserved longer with a little external help, I don't
see why I should put things into my mouth that are on the point
of starting to rot."

"Can I ask you something, Mom? Who's your plastic
surgeon?"

Wincing, his mother gave him a name Borut recognized from
the tabloid media.

"You look good, you know. Much better than him, actually.
I hope you also feel as well as you pay him."

His mother stared at him fixedly, as though unable to decide
whether to accept the compliment or rise to the challenge. Then
she shrugged and stuck her fork in a vegetable. She lifted the
skewered piece and scrutinized it skeptically.

"Like in the old days," she finally said, her voice shaking with
disgust, then she closed her eyes and swallowed.

Borut ate hungrily, for the first time in a long while. The food tasted of food. The man in the back put his arm around the boy's shoulders. He placed a sugar cube between his teeth and showed it to the child, who leaned over to him and took the sugar out of his mouth.

When they put their silverware down, the waiter quickly came to their table. He shook the uneaten vegetables from her plate into a waste separation bag. *Some fifty pork burgers worth of vegetables.* Because the number of Muslims was increasing globally, the price of pork burgers was dropping. Not as fast as the price of real vegetables was rising, but still.

"Would you care for something else?"

Borut shook his head.

"A cup of coffee, sure," said his mother.

The waiter rattled off the coffees on offer, spanning all the continents. At one of the names she stopped him: "That one. With raw cane sugar, please." And looking at Borut: "Two of them."

I could have said no. Children have carried sacks with these coffee beans through the jungle. The price you'll pay for a cup was their wage for twenty-three hours of work. Two eleven-and-a-half hour workdays. A jet of blood pouring into the cup. We'll lift the thick sweet liquid to our lips. The liquid that gives a man the strength to go through whatever the day throws at him. A sip sticks his lips together. He won't talk. He won't yell. And we won't either. You'll dab your lips with a napkin, I'll wipe mine, you'll proffer your cheek for a kiss, I'll quickly brush against it, closing my eyes in discomfort, then we'll leave.

"Good coffee, isn't it?" his mother said.

Borut nodded absent-mindedly.

She leaned closer and asked in confidence:

"Borut, what are you actually doing?"

"I don't know, actually. But it's okay."

"I know you. You've always had to do things your way, ever since you were a toddler. You can't hide it. I had a hard time talking the Chairman into taking you on."

"We all make mistakes."

"Some people can afford to. The Chairman is definitely one

of them. For some it's even part of their image, you know. But what are you going to do now? It seems like you're acting against everything again, even yourself. It won't end well. Things go most smoothly when you just let them run their course."

"I think you've invited the wrong person for lunch, Mom. Monika would've loved this phrase. Her firm makes a living by finding people who'll go with the flow and let things take their course."

"Never mind Monika. I want *you* to be okay."

"But I am okay, Mom."

"Borut. Look at me."

"I am looking at you."

"No. You're looking through me. Look at me. I'd like to tell you something and I want you to listen."

"I am listening, Mom."

"You've tuned out. You tune out too often. You don't listen half the time. That's why things get rocky."

"I'm sorry I'm not to your satisfaction. That's just the way I am."

She shook her head barely perceptibly.

"I'm satisfied with you all right. But—even the mothers of the prophets wanted children, not prophets."

"I don't know what you mean, Mom."

"Never mind. We're done here. I just need to go to the ladies. Oh, before I forget—say hello to Monika for me."

"I will."

"And the little ones, especially the little ones."

"I will." *She still can't remember their names.*

Borut remained seated at the table, watching the man and the child at the table in the back. The man had his arms around the child's shoulders. Sugar cubes glittered in his lap.

It doesn't matter, Mom. If it wasn't me, you'd say: If you won't cooperate, you'll be to blame for the cloning. We can't go on like this. And then it would be harder to say no.

She was gone a long time.

Could something have happened to her?

The waiter approached, discreetly clearing his throat.

"Excuse me, sir, the lady has already settled the bill."

"I see." It took Borut a moment to decipher the hint. "And left?"

"Yes, sir."

"Thank you." He might have sat a little while longer, watching what the man and the child would do next, but the message was unequivocal. He got up and started making his way to the door.

"Thank you, sir. Thank you, please come again." And dropping his voice: "You can always ask for the other menu straight away. We always have something in stock. There's more and more demand."

So things have started to move.

Mom obviously doesn't know that I don't live at home.

If Internal Affairs doesn't know, they obviously won't find me the moment that—

The moment that?

The moment that what?

The moment that anything. *The moment that they start looking for me. For what I have done—or for what I'm going to do.*

No, they won't find me in an instant.

I'll have time to see the children.

12.
Scattered Cha-Cha

I'LL HAVE TIME to see the children.

The dress rehearsal promised the evening would go without a hitch. There wouldn't be a thousand things to sort out before the performance. The realizer—a man Monika had worked with for a long time since she herself never replaced people she was happy with, contrary to the professional advice she gave her clients—would fix a few minor technical hiccups and she could pop home.

She was organizing a presentation of successful intercultural cooperation for a congress of monetary activists that had been transferred to town at the last moment. Fundamentalists had bombed the venue that was originally scheduled, and the corporate people who had arrived early spent the night at the airport and were redirected to the safe heart of a safe town in the heart of a safe country in the heart of a safe continent. The business was not affected; it was conducted via satellites high above the planet, the human resources unnecessary. But it made businesspeople feel more human if they could meet other people on occasion, and the congress provided a good opportunity to convene with their own kind and have a drink with no bad feelings.

The artists hastily patched together a program, which went smoothly nonetheless, except for the role of the African tribal chief dressed in a fake fur costume. This had to be played by a professor of atomic physics, the only black man in town willing to take the role, and he incorporated far too many words like *incompressible fluids, continuous spectrum,* and *hyperfine structure* into his conjuration song and dance, words that somehow didn't seem to fit a tribal chieftain, no matter how vocal the professor was about this being basic terminology that had been wikied so often it was now part of everyday parlance. She would have to speak to him about it before his next performance. The congresses were growing increasingly alike, and Monika knew she would be using this same show again. The problem of reinventing credible identities was the subject of heated debate at all tourism congresses, there were plenty of those and she had something to offer. Identity inventing had been a cash cow for many years now.

Also the reception protocol went well, the congress participants arriving without delay. Ever since the corporate world had started sponsoring the Ministry of Internal Affairs, company presidents were escorted to meetings by squad cars with their sirens on. The same procedure was used on this occasion. Business was becoming stratified; Some managers opted for armored vehicles and bodyguards, others for convertibles and blondes. If I had time, I'd make an analysis of who was who to determine which industry branches had a higher risk factor, thought Monika. That would be a useful stock market tip. She never played the stock market herself, though; it would compromise her credibility if she were ever to suffer a loss and the news got out.

She found out about what papers would be delivered and briefly listened in to a panel discussion on ritual bombings, a thing that could profitably be included in future choreographies, immediately walked away from a tedious discussion on collateral discrimination, and listened to a report on migration trends.

Retired Germans no longer want to remain in Germany because there are too many Turks there. They'd like to go to Thailand, it's beautiful and cheap, except that there are too many Germans there now and it's getting less and less cheap, and it's no longer all that beautiful either, because the most beautiful Thai women have already migrated to Germany. So now they roam the world, not knowing where to invest the last years of their lives. They are unhappy.

I'd solve their problem in a blink of an eye. Impose exit taxes that are steep enough, and they'll happily stay at home.
At home.
At home I'll pretend I'm not at home. I'll hide. Otherwise the children might start crying, they might want me to stay and I can't stay.

The card unlocked the door noiselessly. She peeked from behind the door, her movement masked by noisy music the babysitter had selected. They hadn't noticed her arrival, *it's possible to be both here and absent at the same time, an ideal combination.*

The boys were blindly trying to break the various security codes, but they had all been changed since the last hacking. The babysitter was making herself a snack from the overfilled fridge. They always called the same girl. They didn't replace people they were satisfied with. An anthropology student. Quiet and efficient. She would tell the boys stories she made up herself. Stories about timid gods and courageous children. The boys would listen with large eyes that gradually filled with sleep. Even Borut would sometimes stand outside the door and listen, before they went out.

A pity he hadn't slept with her every now and then, I saw the way she looked at him. Sure, a well-preserved intellectual, rebellious, eats healthy food, mysteriously keeps to his room, and a fatherly type to boot. It could have happened, easily. He might not have left in that case. Change can be soothing.

"Bedtime, boys!" the sitter clapped her hands.

"If you tell us how the World Bank ate Africa!" the boys demanded in unison.

Well-coordinated interests. Hmm, I don't know this story. What do they tell them in preschool?

"Again? Always the same one?"

"It's so scary!"

"Oh, all right. But only if you brush your teeth and slip under the covers."

"We will but—"

"No but, unless you want the *I'd-tell-you-a-story-but!*"

"What do you mean *slip*?"

The sitter laughed.

"You'll hear in the story. The exchange rate slipped, the money slipped into the President's account, the President slipped into another country, half of the continent slipped into the pockets of the big boys from the World Bank . . . Don't miss it now, seeing as you were unable to be part of it then!"

"We won't, we won't," they yelled, making a mad dash for the bathroom.

Monika was not quick enough to get out of their way.

"Mommy. Did you just come or are you just leaving?"

"I'd left, but I've come back."

"Uh-huh."

"But I'm leaving again. I have to."

"Uh-huh. We knew that. Have a nice time. See ya."

Monika was looking for some words of closure, but unwilling to wait that long, the boys had already climbed into their beds.

They manage well without him. And they also manage—without me.

The babysitter appeared from the kitchen. Her sandwich looked like a sloppily planned apartment building, the layers clumsily following one another.

Borut wouldn't want to sleep with her. There's mayo and sausage in her sandwich.

"Is everything all right?" she asked, obviously wondering whether she should hide her sandwich or not.

Shouldn't I be asking her this?

"Everything's fine, I just popped home, I'm in a rush, but there's something I had to—I've forgotten something."

What was that again? To check on the boys?

"I'm just putting them to bed."

"I heard. Teeth, story, and all that. Sure. Carry on."

The babysitter nodded.

"But eat first. They'll wait."

A person works better on a full stomach.

If I told that to my clients they'd terminate the contract.

The sitter looked at the sandwich she was carrying as though she had no idea how it had gotten there.

"Hypermarket food," she said eventually.

Right? Wrong?

"Not the best quality, I know," said Monika uncertainly, "but my husband's away, he normally does the grocery shopping—"

The sitter sunk her teeth into the construction.

"Okay. No child labor," she said. "Guaranteed. With those privately-owned farms you never know when they make their children do these things. Butcher animals, for instance," she said in reply to Monika's confused look.

"And you think that—" said Monika hesitantly. *What do I think she thinks?*

"I think that's not right. Let them stay children. They can slaughter things later, after—"

After they grow up. And have to do it. If not animals, then—

"Well, I digress a bit, ma'am. You go on, I'll finish eating when the kids are asleep. No need to rush back, I've brought a lot of work." She motioned toward a stack of books on the dining table. Monika scanned a few titles: *Ritual Slaughtering in Pre-Capitalist Society. Beware of Thy Neighbor as Thyself. God is Loss.* "Time to finish my degree."

"Sure." Then Monika realized she was possibly expected to continue. "If you have any trouble finding a job—"

The sitter shook her head.

"I won't be looking for a job. Beware that, when fighting monsters, you yourself do not become a monster."

"I don't quite understand that," said Monika slowly.

"Nietzsche. *Beyond Good and Evil.* Then there's the bit about the abyss, but I don't think that's all that important. Philosophers talk too much. We need action."

"I know, I took an exam in Nihilism 101. But—"

"The connection? Everything's connected. Nothing is random and unintentional."

"But—"

What are we talking about now? Nihilism? Anthropology? Globalism? Terrorism? Street riots? Human resources?

"Didn't you say you were in a hurry?" the sitter interrupted.

"Oh, right, of course. I'm leaving, sorry."

Sorry?

"That's all right." The sitter came closer and held the door open for her.

That's all right?

When she walked into the banquet hall, she had a mild anxiety attack. *There are more people than we were told, the waiters are not refilling their glasses quickly enough, the gourmet foods aren't presented well, some of the tables are utterly bare, the lights are too bright, poor interpersonal flow, I can sense a feeling of weariness permeating the room—*

Then girls wearing dental floss came in, bringing energy drinks. The atmosphere loosened up, she walked around, nodding hello and exchanging a few words with the people she knew. Having done her dutiful rounds, she finally relaxed and took an unknown orange beverage, *a verified provider, I'd never take something unknown in a bar, apparently some bars add more and more hallucinogens to their drinks, and others, truth serums, how can one continue to do business—*

"Good evening, how are you?"

"Fine, thanks. And you?"

"Very well, thank you."

No need to talk anymore. Just listen.

"We'll have to go on."

"We're moving to another place."

"I hear things are moving."

"Listen to your inner voice."

"I would, but it keeps objecting."

"It's important to know how to respond to an objection."

"Have you bought anything lately?"

"We have, a lot. What about you?"

"We have. It feels like a lot."

"Buying is a feeling. A good feeling."

"Good. Our patents are good. I think."

"Patented ideas are more expensive, but reliable. You know what you're getting."

"For those who can afford them."

"You can afford to splash out."

"A few billion, don't gloat."

"Basically, I don't envy you."

"Have you done anything basically wrong?"

"Basically, no."

"Rumor has it that you essentially took over."

"Essentially, we may have."

"If I sum up his words, this is really a different matter."

"He really didn't say anything."

"I briefly understood that."

"In brief, we are where we are, and as we are."

"It's nice here, isn't it?"

"Nice airport, nice hotel."

"We had a nice arrival."

"I'm glad I've finally made it to Casinoland."

"I've heard a lot about it, but one has to see it for oneself."

"It's the sign of times, don't trust anyone."

"I'll drink to that."

"Good evening, Monika."

Who's that again?

Oh right, the head of the organizing committee. The client. We did all the work through intermediaries—

"Good evening," she said. *Should I call him by his name? Have we ever shaken hands? Do we usually do that? Have I been drinking the wrong thing?*

"It is a good evening, indeed," said the man.

He likes it. He's complacent.

"Is everything all right? Are you happy?"

The man's brow furrowed.

Surprised? Wondering?

"Of course everything's all right, Monika. Could it be any different with you in charge? And of course I'm happy. Is there another option?"

Monika nodded.

"I'm glad to hear that," she said. "And now—"

"Now we can have a quiet drink in my office, just the two of us,"

"—if you'll excuse me, I have to go home, my kids are waiting for me. I'm in a rush. Our sitter is an apprentice terrorist."

"Ah. I see," said the man, confused.

I'm glad. That means it's possible.

Happy stories are not interesting.

What does the world get from a person who doesn't see the world?

Everyone satisfied. Everyone victorious. Everyone proud of themselves.

I'm going to be sick.

Uninteresting.

But that's what I do.

Now she knew.

This was the world from which Borut had long been gone.

13.
Horizontal Pogo

THIS WAS THE world from which Borut had long been gone.

He looked at it in disbelief.

The same as before. The same. I've left and nothing has changed. Outwardly.

On the inside, everything's different.

That store—to think of all the things I've bought there. How little I really needed them. All the times I sat at those tables by the river. All the things I said just because I didn't want silence to speak up. And all the times I walked along this embankment, thinking. Working things out in my mind. Things that had happened. Things that would happen. Misunderstanding everything.

The embankment.

It's dangerous on the embankment. Things flow here. People discharging and taking in liquids. So much water so close to home. It seems like everything could be washed away. The river—always the same yet always changing. Up and down, past every obstacle.

The ATM in the passageway across from the store entrance was rusting. Anthropologists were launching discussions on the need to protect the cultural heritage of cash payments.

The entrance to their building was the same. The same securely locked door, the same buzzers. Maybe his name was no longer on the buzzer, but he was too far away to worry about it. The same. And yet everything was different now; he couldn't go in now.

Monika will collect the children from preschool just before closing time. They'll drive up around seven.

He checked the time.

I still have my watch. I can still sell my watch. And the car. If I sell the car, I'll have nothing left. Completely free.

He checked the time.

Almost seven.

He checked the time.

They'll drive up.

They'll see me.

The boys will cry out.

I won't be able to resist.

I'll run to them.

Monika will yell at me. What have I done. How dare I.

Then she'll remember that people could be watching. That people are sure to be watching.

She'll fall silent.

She'll give me a hug.

So that people could see.

The boys will see.

I won't be able to push her away and run down to the embankment and on, away.

I need to get out of the way.

I need to hide.

There, behind those dumpsters. They won't look that way. Nobody looks that way, ever.

It's safe here. Here I can see everything, and nobody'll see me.

Where are they? It's past seven. Preschool's closed.

What am I doing? Hiding behind dumpsters, here, outside my—

What now? Where to now?

Something moved among the dumpsters.

Every time I stuff some garbage in one, I can hear the bones of tiny animals cracking—

Somebody touched his arm.

He turned.

Not them. Thank god.

He'd seen this man before. Many times. Right here.

"This spot's taken," the man told him.

"Excuse me?"

"One bum's all this place can take, says the guy from the council. An' that bum's me. You go find yourself someplace else."

Borut was at a loss.

"No, I'm not—"

The homeless man took a step backward.

"Oh, right, it's you. Sorry. Didn't recognize ya. You look kinda worse for wear, if you know what I mean. Thought you was competition. You know how it goes. You gotta protect your turf."

Well, I'm doing fine. This one already sees me as one of his own.

"I'm sorry, I have no money left."

"No sweat. I know how it goes. You don't give nothing for years, then you give three times what the others give. It doesn't add up. You gotta move slow or you get derailed."

I can hardly argue with that. Do I have to? Do I lose my dignity if I agree with—him?

"You got knocked sideways, didn't ya? No need to tell me if you don't want to. I know anyway."

"How do you know?"

"I see everything, I know everything, and I don't tell nothing. Ah, screw it. You walked out and left the kids with the broad. Now you feel bad and you wanna see how they're doing. You ain't the first like that. But you're something else. You went *on a mission.*"

He stopped and looked at him.

"You're something else. Most guys leave the kids with the broad because of some other broad, not because of some *mission.*"

"My kids are not the only kids in the world. There are others too. And they also deserve—"

Monika would have felt differently. It's our children that matter. Let other people take care of other children.

The homeless man put a finger to his mouth.

"Congratulations," he said. "Welcome to the club."

Club?

"What club?"

"There is no actual club, that's just a metaphor. The club of us people with children of our own. Who nonetheless care about other children. In that sense."

Now he's talking differently. We're in the same club. Before—that was just pretense. All the time we've been meeting we were both playing our parts. Outwardly. This now—this is for real. He's taken me in.

"Do you have children too?"

The homeless man nodded.

"Of course."

"So then we do have something in common."

"We do. And not only that."

"What else?"

"We're both against."

Against?

"Against?"

"Against. And we're not the only ones."

Against what?

"Against what?"

The man stepped close, very close.

His smell—there's nothing unpleasant about his smell. There should be, but there isn't. There is no smell at all.

"Against things being the way they are. Take this, for example, it may sound a little pompous, but I like it nevertheless: Against exploitation. For instance, the exploitation of the world for the sake of God. Or the exploitation of God for secular purposes."

He nodded to himself.

"And we're not the only ones. There are others."

"What others?"

"Others who are against."

"I don't see them—"

There may be. But they're not here. Not in this street. Not behind these dumpsters. And I never saw them at parties thrown by the rich when I still used to attend.

"There are."

"Others? Like you?"

"And like yourself."

"Are you—are you some secret organization?"

He could feel the homeless man eyeing him. He could feel his own organs, the beat of his heart, the peristalsis in his digestive tract, the pressure in his lungs, the flow of blood in his veins, his lung alveoli grabbing and chewing oxygen. *I'm alive. That's the message.*

"The era of secret organizations is over. Opus Dei? Freemasons? Rosicrucians? Adepts? Kids' stuff. It's easy to join a system that's already in place. Now is the time of the secret individual."

Secret. Behind the garbage. With a council-issued pass. A deployed beggar. If you misbehave, you get recalled. That kind of time.

"And what is he secretive about?"

"The same as you and I. Himself. We've hidden from people. But we're making a mistake. By hiding ourselves we are also hiding our message."

"And what is this message?"

I'd really like to hear it. It's mine too.

The man smiled.

"Words are unnecessary. Our life is our message."

I've heard this before—

"Words help," said Borut uncertainly.

"If they help, let's hear them. Tell me your story."

Why should I tell it to the first person I meet in the street, oh, sorry, by the dumpsters? If I really felt like telling my story, I'd choose someone I've known a long time—

Easy. Easy.

Wrong direction.

You tried to tell someone you've known a long time. Longer than anyone else.

She didn't take you seriously.

"I can tell you. Everything from the beginning. But—"

"Don't worry, I have time."

Borut talked for a long time, not leaving anything out, remembering everything, from the first sketched outlines on paper down to the last fruit peel in the refugee center, from the first money transfers to the last rotten teeth in the mouths of passersby. He talked for a long time, and the homeless man listened. Toward the end—*should I stop here or go on and tell him what I intend to do now?*—he began to wonder whether his story made sense. *Would anyone believe it if they read it on a screen?*

The man was nodding. Looking at Borut as though he was

trying to decide whether to tell him what was on his mind or not. Finally, he asked.

"You do realize that Synthesis is adding vitamins and all those, like, healthy additives to its plastic, don't you?"

"Adding?"

"Of course. It's strange they never told you that when you were writing their ads. There was plenty of opportunity for extra word play: No need to eat a whole crate of apples, we've put enough vitamins in a single one. Stuff like that."

"But then why—"

"Well. Vitamin intake is not the problem. All sorts of stuff is now being added to food, you know, if you read the small print you'll see it's healthier than ever. It's just that, as the old exploitative adage says, too much of a good thing is bad for you."

"I don't understand."

"Side effects. The body hasn't been able to adapt to the speed of the progress. It's saturated with vitamins, a vitamin overdose if you like, the external enemy is eliminated, the immune system goes on vacation, and in come the autoimmune diseases. The immune system attacks the body. Because the synthesized plants are so pumped full of vitamins, the body no longer needs to fight the external enemy and finds one within. And it's of course much less prepared for this battle, so the consequences are far worse, you know civil wars are the worst bloodbaths, one just doesn't expect an attack from within. I don't know whether I should go into detail—"

"But how come the poor people are affected more? Rich people can still afford real vegetables—"

"The poor have a harder time concealing what they're missing. Don't tell me you still have all of your teeth? Or that your wife doesn't use skins creams and treatments? Have you ever tallied up how much these things cost and thought about the average income? Yes, differences do show, preservation comes at a price. And the same goes for nutritional habits. Where there's a lot of new stuff, old things increase in value, and not everyone can afford the new prices. And besides, autoimmune diseases thrive on a similar genetic makeup. And so does poverty."

"Come on. Poverty is not hereditary."

"Not directly. But you know about the movement between social strata yourself. Yes, I realize I'm generalizing, but think of how you generalized things! You acted by rote, unthinkingly, going by what you learned in preschool. But you're no longer in preschool. You didn't research the causes and effects."

"Are you saying—"

"That you're not doing much for the health of humanity by occasionally replacing artificial fruit with the real thing. What you did was good in itself, it makes people feel better about themselves if they see someone's concerned about their welfare, but—well, you know what I mean."

Borut started laughing. "So I've given away all my money for the wrong cause?"

A fatal error, perhaps? Very funny. Apparently.

"It's not the end of the world. The money felt good circulating, that's its purpose. And a real apple never hurt anybody. If nothing else, a person who can tell the difference finds the taste more natural."

Borut nodded.

"And besides—if you want things to be natural, surely you can't find it natural that half of the world's population lives on less money a day than you pay for a cup of coffee. By giving away what you had you just lessened the difference a bit, didn't you?"

Borut nodded.

"Everything you don't give is lost, I've also heard say. You're doing just fine. If you need money, I'll get some for you," said the homeless man irritably. "But now slow down a bit in giving it away, okay? Haste is dangerous."

"God ostensibly took seven days to create the world, I took me two months to—"

To what? Tear down mine?

"That's what I'm saying. Too fast."

The man looked over Borut's shoulder and nodded. Borut turned around. Monika ran from her car to the steps to the building.

She's forgotten to collect the boys from preschool. Maybe she's forgotten I'm gone—

"The babysitter's there."

Why did she come home so early in that case?

"She just wants to see the children. She won't stay long."

See the children? Monika kept whining about not having enough time with the kids, but in reality she didn't know what to do with them.

"And she'll see them. And you'll see them some other time."

What other time, there may not be another time—

"What else were you going to do today aside from catching a glimpse of your boys from a distance?"

Borut took a deep breath.

This man has been here all the time. Outside my building. Watching me. Forming ideas.

Knowing everything.

If he knows everything, he also knows this.

And if he doesn't know?

If he knows everything, he should also know this.

"Attack Synthesis. Destroy it, if possible."

It shouldn't be there, it's not right. It should be removed.

If not it, then me.

That's what I've been thinking about all the time.

Both these things.

They're related.

"If you can't join 'em, beat 'em? Fine, okay, but—why? Even if you did destroy it—they'd just build another factory. The profits are beyond belief."

"As payback for what it's done to me."

Even if it's not as dangerous as I thought—it's a symbol. A symbol invading every human body.

"What, given you money?"

"Made me guilty, to blame."

And it's easier to blame Synthesis rather than myself, I have to admit that.

"Because you were part of it?

"I'm ashamed of having been a part of it."

If you can't change the fate of the majority you have to share it. And I don't want that. I want to drink tap water. Eat natural fruit.

The kind with less vitamins, ha ha. The kind that rots and doesn't bounce off the floor.

"There's no need for that. That's part of the deal. You can renounce society, but to do that you first have to be part of society. Enough talk, though. Let's be specific. You'll have a hard time getting in. It's sealed airtight. So that fruit won't start cross-fertilizing inside."

"I don't understand."

"You know. The birds and the bees and all that. As soon as you introduce the human factor, things get complicated. For as long as humanity has existed, it has striven to grow taller, faster, stronger vegetables. But there are limits. After a certain point it no longer seems good. Four-meter long bananas wouldn't sell. Things need to be kept under control. That's why Synthesis is an unmanned factory."

The human factor eliminated? The Chairman would love that. He's probably a stockholder—

The Chairman. Whatever happened to him?

Doesn't matter.

The homeless man was watching him and Borut motioned for him to continue.

"And even if you managed to get in, you do realize there are backup systems in Synthesis, don't you? A system like that can't be brought to its knees just like that."

"I know there is no other way. But I also know what they don't know. That a person can interfere. You said it yourself. People bring uncertainty. That's what I want."

"I see. But it won't affect Synthesis. It's a next generation factory. It self-regenerates."

Self-regenerates? Like evil in superhero movies? Something here escaped from the world of science fiction, like a projection of the future that has gone too far—

"Self-regenerates? As in it regenerates itself? How is that possible?"

"Like nature. The same as nature. Synthesis and nature substitute for one another. That's why it's blended in so well with its surroundings. If you weren't actually looking for a factory, you wouldn't spot it. That's why it can keep growing."

Cities that feed on refuse. The holy grail of 21st century architecture.

"How do you know?"

The homeless man smiled.

"I built those systems. I know how they work."

Borut leaned against a dumpster.

Something's moving about inside.

Don't look in. If you look in, it'll pull you inside.

If there's something in there, it can crawl out.

This teeming . . . someone should see to—

Someone else.

I've had enough for—

This evening? A lifetime?

"And now you're here."

"That's why. To redeem my guilt."

These are my words, I was supposed to say that.

We're in the same club.

"And if you know how it works you also know—"

The homeless man waited.

I need to go on, I'll go on.

"—how to stop it."

The homeless man waited. Pondered.

"Beware the one who knows how, because he also knows he's right," he said slowly. "I know it can't be stopped. There are things that get out of hand."

I know all about that as well. The hammer and sickle, the sickle in the poster, the sickle in the knee.

"But I also know where the heart of the system is."

Borut nodded.

"That's where I want to go. The heart of the matter."

And then let happen whatever will.

"You'll find nothing special there. I've told you—it can't be stopped. There is, however, another thing. Something I've considered myself. Synthesis will sense that it's not the only one there. That there's life *not* created by it. And then—then things may shift. It's not programmed to ignore intrusion. It's only programmed to fix the consequences."

"So what happens then?"

"Then? I don't know. I do know what happens if we don't do this."

We. Plural. No more solitude. We've become partners.

He's been thinking about it. Waiting for someone to come along who'd be willing to go in.

"If we don't do it, things will just go on as before. On and on. We have to go in."

"Yeah, but how do I get in? If it's sealed airtight?"

"Like any other place. Through the door."

"It doesn't open for just anyone."

"No, of course not. It's secure. Fingerprint access."

"So I guess it won't open for me."

"So I guess I'll be coming with you. I have to get my thumb in this pie. The door shall open."

"And once I'm in, what then?"

"What indeed? You know yourself. The control room. That's where the heart of the system is. If you were to jam something metal into the right spot there—"

"Something metal?"

"Here you go. This'll do."

Borut saw what his new partner was proffering.

Dulce and Gibboni for Aleksia, 2005. A collectible.

"I had one just like—"

"I know."

I had this one.

"Just jam it into a main frame node."

The cold of the metal in his palm restored balance.

It's all becoming more solid.

"Are you coming with me? Inside?"

The man smiled.

"In spirit. You'll manage on your own. Right where it says SEED. It can hardly go on without seed."

"Seed?"

"Don't laugh. It's an acronym for Standard Equivalent Energy Distribution. You should be happy the thing has a name. All the other boards only have generic markings. A confusion of letters and digits. A name, that's better. More specific. Remember that."

"I'll remember it. What about you?"

"Me? I can forget about it now. You've come along, so my work is done."

"No, I don't mean that. What's your name?"

The homeless man smiled.

"You don't need to know my name. You'll find me if you need me."

Borut nodded. "This is not the last time we'll see each other."

The old man nodded.

"It's not," he said.

The corkscrew slid into the node without a hitch.

He was showered by a splash of sparks.

Electric current rushed through his body.

The corkscrew rattled down the control panel and across the floor to the door.

It's done its part, it can stay here.
I have to take it, I have to get it out, it's a clue.
It doesn't matter.
It doesn't matter for you. It matters for Monika and the children.
They'll track them down. It's a rarity. A collectible.

A fascinating experience, he thought later, when his shaking tissues stabilized a bit. All his internal organs had resonated, tautened, shuddered, called attention to themselves, each one in turn, and his heart went on beating in a very singular rhythm for a long time. He looked at the corkscrew and considered having another go at it. If he gripped it less firmly, the danger would be less—it would be ripped out of his hand more quickly. He looked at the corkscrew and listened to his pancreas, his liver, his kidneys, his gut—what do they feel? What do they want? Do they still want to be with him, are they still willing to cooperate, or would they prefer to be elsewhere and that he manage on empty?

Are they with me or aren't they?

He looked at the corkscrew in his hand.

Let's do it again. It feels good, this new feeling.

The control panel was still spurting and crackling. The stench of melting plastic was burning in his nostrils.

Leave it be, go away. It's done. What had to be done. You'll continue when you have to. You can go back now.

Back.

The night was pressing down, people were swarming out of the office buildings. A serpent of light flashed above Synthesis, high up into the sky, carrying the smell of melted silicon with it.

The flame was huge, reaching in its might from earth to heaven, that's what they would've said in the old days.

That was in the old days. Now nothing reaches from earth to heaven.

People glanced at the flame, shrugged, and went home.

Nobody notices me.

Nobody notices the flame. Nobody knows Synthesis is on fire. Nobody knows anything's on fire.

And if somebody does know there's a fire, who knows that the thing burning is Synthesis?

It will eat its own flame. Absorb it.

Tomorrow there'll be plenty of fried bananas and fried peppers in the stores.

What are the retailers going to do with fried watermelons?

The owners won't like it; a product shouldn't change that drastically that quickly.

Perhaps a good advertising campaign will show the increased health benefits of melted plastic—

Stop.

You've put Synthesis behind you now, it's over and done with.

Your work is done. You've proven that you can. To yourself. You're free again now.

Like in books.

And it was night and it was morning, a new day.

14.
Solitary Paso Doble

AND IT WAS night and it was morning, a new day.

The boys didn't want to go to preschool.

"It's better at home," they told Monika. "You're home too."

"Don't you have to go to work anymore?" the elder one asked her straight out.

"How are we going to get money now?" the younger one was terrified.

"Daddy said we have some savings," the interrogation went on.

"Do we have enough to go on being a happy family?"

"Ema said that children have to work in some societies."

"Will we have to go to work now that you're home?"

Ema—who's Ema? Oh, right, the anthropologist babysitter. I could call her.

"No, you won't have to go to work."

For the time being.

"Good. What about preschool?"

"I don't know. Won't you be bored at home with all the play machines locked?"

"They're locked all the time anyway. You can play with us."

"Me?"

I can't—

"We'll teach you, don't worry."

I won't know how, I'm too old—

The doorbell rang. *Who could that be, we haven't ordered anything, why did Borut refuse to have a videophone installed—*

Borut?

"Who is it?"

"Vladimir."

Vladimir? Who—

Ooh. Vladimir.

"I'll come down," she said. And to the children: "Set everything up, I'll be back in a minute."

She ran downstairs, wondering whether she should open the door wide enough to let him in the lobby. *But then maybe I won't be able to push him out again and the boys are waiting for me upstairs—*

She stepped outside, on the stoop, in front of the row of buzzers. He was waiting, leaning against the wall.

Perhaps I should've taken some papers with me, to make it look like he was here on some work-related business.

Stop it. This hide-and-seek is no longer important. Not anymore. Not for you.

"You again."

"Yes."

"I see you've learned how to find at least one thing in town."

"Yes. The way from me to you."

A long way, longer than you think.

"So you just dropped by? To see how I was doing? That's nice."

"Well, no, not quite—"

"You've come to show me that those little girls haven't eaten you alive?"

"Girls eaten me alive? Oh, those. I left soon, we couldn't find a common language. But you were no longer on the bench."

But I was no longer on the bench. He went back to the bench. To see if I was still there.

"What then?"

"I came to say goodbye."

Goodbye?

"Is something the matter?"

"I received some news from home."

"Yes?"

"My grandfather died."

"Oh. I'm sorry. But it was to be expected, wasn't it? How old was he again? Close to a hundred?"

"Close, yes."

"Well, I would've loved to ask him how you get to be that old." *Would I really?* "I'm sorry. My manners are awful, I know. When it comes to death. I have a problem with death."

Vladimir almost smiled.

"I guess we all do. When the time comes."

What is he saying? That for me the time has already come when I have a right to have a problem with death?

He hesitated.

"There's another thing—"

"What other thing?"

"My father's been found."

Have we talked about his father too? No, we skipped Dad—

"What happened to your father?"

"He disappeared."

"When?"

"Fifteen years ago."

Fifteen years ago? You were the same age as my kids, one of my kids, I don't even know how old you are—

"And? Where was he found?"

"In a pit somewhere."

"Dead?"

Vladimir nodded.

"And they're sure it's him?"

"So they say."

"They say? After fifteen years? Who identified him? Your mother?"

"My mother also died."

"Now?"

Stupid. You're supposed to ask—when?

"No. Back then."

"When?"

"When my father went missing."

"What happened to her?"

"I don't know. I was too small."

I wasn't told.

He wasn't told.

"Vladimir! What kind of a family is that? What happened to your people? They just went missing—"

"Every family has its share of troubles," said Vladimir dryly.

Don't go poking into mine. You have your own.

"Uh-huh. And now you're all alone."

"All alone. My grandfather held out for a long time."

Waiting for Dad to be found.

"They didn't get along, my father and him, but still. You know how it is."

You have kids of your own.

"So what are you going to do now?"

"I have to leave now. Two funerals at once. I can go. Back. Where I belong. I have a place now. An empty place."

"Different than before?"

"Different. Before, I wanted to burn my passport. And stay here. Help out here."

"Are you insane? Burn your passport? That means burn yourself. You'd be left without an identity. Do you understand that?"

Like—like those people who rummage through garbage. In India. Perhaps also here. I don't know. I don't ask their names, if I ever even see them.

Vladimir nodded.

"I wouldn't be the first person to do that."

"I mean, nobody here knows who you are. Nobody knows your name. Nobody except—"

She fell silent.

He could also stay here. Become somebody else. Start over. Do anything.

"You're going back? What are you going to do there?"

"Do?"

"Well, you're alone now. Say, how are you going to make a living? No mom, no dad, no grandfather. Do you have any brothers or sisters?"

Vladimir shook his head.

"What can you do? What did you study to do?"

What I went to school for doesn't require studying.

"I can play the guitar."

Monika made a deprecating gesture.

"The guitar?"

Even Borut no longer touched the guitar, and he was much older than Vladimir. The guitar's history, he said. Now music is made by touching keys. And icons. Virtually.

"There have been so many guitarists, you know. Jimi Hendrix, Brian Jones, Kurt Cobain . . ."

She stopped.

"Do you know them?"

He nodded.

"For sure. I just don't know why you've only named dead ones. The ones that died young."

What are you trying to tell me? That you have to die to be taken seriously? Like my dad did? Like my grandpa didn't do?

Why? Because they came to mind.

"They came to mind. Their pictures are on T-shirts. It kind of goes together with an idol to die young. If somebody came to my office and said they wanted to become an idol, that's the first thing I'd advise them to do—die. If it weren't too late already. Idols die young. Christ too."

"Christ did *not* die young. He died—"

"At thirty-three."

"I'm sorry. How old are you?"

"More than that."

"And you're still alive."

"So I obviously won't become an idol. There are other options."

I'll have to choose some other option than the present one.

"Well, there are options for me too. I can do things. You'll see. You could come with me."

"I can't."

"Why not?"

"I have kids."

I know.

I know you know.

"I'll take care of the children as if they were my own. Believe me."

"You're—"

You're just a child yourself.

"I will."

"The boys. They're waiting for me, upstairs, alone. I have to go."

He moved away from the wall, stepped closer to her.

Should I step back? Forward?

"You haven't fallen in love with me."

"I haven't."

I'll fall in love when you're gone. It's safer that way.

"I thought—"

I wasn't thinking. Had I been thinking, I wouldn't have come. Not the first time, not now.

"Take it easy. It just happened. I'm not sorry it did. But it can't go on."

We've both said our big words. Now what? Do we cry?

"Go, then. Your kids are waiting, remember."

"Don't be sad. It's not that I don't—"

It's not that I don't love you. As much as I know how. And as much as I can, next to Borut and myself.

"I'm not sad. It's just that—"

Of course I'm sad. It's just that.

"—It's just that I always want to be some place where I'm not. I spent the whole night in my room thinking that I wanted to be at your place. So I came here. And now I want to go away. Before, when they tried to tie me to them, I wanted to run away. And now that my grandfather's gone I want to be with him. You're grown up, do you understand this?"

If only the children weren't at home, if only I'd packed them off to preschool—

"I understand. I'll tell you a story I was once told by my—"

I was on the point of saying ex, but—

"—my husband."

Vladimir said quietly:

"Where is your husband, Monika?"

"I don't know."

"When did he leave?"

"I don't know."

I know when I last saw him, that morning before the fries on the floor and the milk under the table, but—he'd left long before that. When? I don't know.

"And why did he leave?"

I don't know.

"Sometimes things happen so that other things can happen. You met me so that you can meet the one after me. So that whatever starts happening when you meet her will seem real."

Just as you happened to me so that I can be alone. And not be afraid. This is the point I needed to reach. Now anything's possible again. Falling in love, whether it's an illusion or not, is some kind of rebirth, it reawakens the atoms slowly smothered by the long years of monotony.

"The story," said Vladimir.

"The story," repeated Monika. "Told to me by my husband. A guy who came back from prison told him what they used to tell each other there: 'There's this guy who's in jail, but he dreams of being a king and living in utter royal luxury every single night, no exception, while far away from the prison there's a king who dreams just the opposite dream every night, of being in prison, and he lives thinking about jail. Which one is happier?' And the answer: 'The prisoner in the winter, the king in the summer.'"

The point of this story is that the reality of a given situation doesn't really matter, Borut would add needlessly. *When a person lives happily it doesn't matter at all whether their happiness is based on reality or imagination.*

Students of advertising would surely clap.

But.

But then you left. And wrote to me: Happiness built on a lie. Is that right?

Vladimir was silent for a long time.

"Thank you," he said.

Monika nodded.

Who is it that doesn't have to say thank you?

"I have a story too. It happened to me."

"Tell me."

"When I left those airbrains in the park, you were gone from the bench. But there were two men close by. Older men. Close to the end."

People who've lost their jobs, people who never had jobs—

"They were yelling at each other, I didn't understand the language. Then they drew knives."

Monika groaned. Vladimir shook his head, placing a hand on hers.

A warm, familiar feeling.

"It wasn't a big deal. I'm used to knives."

Back home boys fight with knives a lot, they're good at it, and the knives are kept sharp. A knife fight is the pinnacle of growing up, and death from a knife is a death we'd choose or dream of if we could choose or dream of our own death.

"But. The blades weren't open. It was like they wanted to stab each other in secret. Back home a knife in the hand means showing off: Look at me, look what I can do!"

And this fight was harassment, they didn't get involved in it to show what they could do, to show that they had no fear of the blade, but to humiliate one another, to show to the other how scared he actually was.

"And? What did you do?"

"I watched. They flailed about in the air a little. Neither of them dared come too close. So that he wouldn't be sliced open. Then one of them shouted: 'What are you looking at?'"

"And what did you say?"

"A knife is real. You only die once. You have to die the right way."

"And what did they do?"

"They realized it wasn't the right way. They put away their knives."

Maybe it wasn't the way that felt wrong, maybe it was the timing.

"Naturally one wants to avoid pain. But. Pride comes from learning to embrace it. If you circle too far from the knife, that makes you a coward. If you come close—and survive—"

He paused.

"—you're stronger. Pain—brings you closer. To yourself. You feel where you are, what you are."

I know. That's why I'm afraid.

Pain is closeness.

What did I feel the first time I slept with—the man whose name Borut won't remember?

What did I feel the first time I slept with Borut?

What did I feel when I did what I did with you?

What did I feel when I gave birth? The first time, the second time? It hurt. And it was beautiful. Intense.

Oh, I spend far too much time around young people. I've come to think like girls that ritually slash their wrists.

"Staying here," said Vladimir slowly, "would be nice, but easy. Now I know I have to be whatever I will be there. There's a place there. For me. Here—here I'm only running away. And I can't run anymore."

He paused and gave her a look.

"Gotta find my destiny, before it gets too late."

"Those are some very important sounding words," said Monika, confused. *Too late, for you?*

"It's a song," he said quickly. "I'm not really sure what it means. It's full of important sounding words, also about some disease and cure, but I don't know what it all means."

Monika laughed. Vladimir looked at her and she fell silent.

"Someone who's ill probably understands," he said.

"Probably."

I really should go—

"I'll be all right," he said. "I hope you'll be all right too."

She nodded.

Sure I'll be all right. Is there another option?

When she was walking up the stairs it occurred to her: *We didn't hug. And we could have.*

The children never noticed she'd been gone more than a minute. They were playing by themselves, another set of game pieces waiting by the side of the board. "I'll be with you in a moment," she said. They didn't so much as nod, let alone ask about preschool. The dice rolled on the board.

Another message from Borut had arrived.

Monika, I'm sorting things out. I'm not finished yet, but I'm making progress.

I know you'll immediately say—what about us? It might be easier if we no longer thought about us. If we started over. I'm different. What about you? A person can change. Every new love teaches you that you were wrong about what love was before. But what we had was good. And if I'm not there, it doesn't mean I'm not close.

I miss the boys, Monika. What had to be done is over. I'd like to come see them. When they come home from preschool. If they went to preschool today. I'll come home. About seven. I still have the card.

You know: It'll be easier if you're not there. Thanks for under-standing. Let me know what time you're coming back, what time I should leave.

I'm all right. I hope you'll be too.

Yes, Borut. I'll be all right too.

"This is Monika."

Her assistant paused for a second.

"Monika, could you call back a little later, please?"

Was she always that standoffish?

The office is so far, far away. I no longer know. Probably she just seems that way. And I wouldn't have wanted to be too friendly with someone that—

"I just wanted—"

"Please call back a bit later. I'm very busy at the moment."

It's my business so even if you're busy, in reality it's me who's busy—

No.

Me too.

I too am busy. The other kind of busy, the more important kind.

"It won't take long. Whatever you're busy with can wait."

The assistant drew in a sharp breath, then cleared her throat and said with all the calm she had learned to muster at commu-nication training:

"Go ahead."

It's her business, that's what she thought now. Maybe, if I'm good, a fraction of it will be mine in a few years, and then, bit by bit—

"I'm leaving. I'm leaving you in charge of the business for a while."

"I—"

I already am.

"Yes?"

She was going to say, I already am.

"Nothing, go ahead."

But she doesn't dare yet.

"Please forward my share of the profits to the Bank of Antarctica account."

Just in case. In case Borut locks the family accounts. I would if I could. But I haven't memorized the codes.

"Monika! How can I—Where are you going?"

I was silent.

Right. Where am I going?

There was only one right answer.

"Against the flow."

I have until about six o'clock, I decided. I sorted out my things. Bought the essentials. Switched off my communicators after deleting the histories. Checked the total in my checking account. Cooked food. It wasn't as difficult as I'd thought. The boys taught me some of their games. Some of them are quite fun. I'll probably remember a few.

The evening was approaching. I told the boys I was leaving. They asked me if I'd be gone long. I said I didn't know, but that they'd be alone for only a little while. I gave them a new box of building blocks, which they immediately dove into. I stood by the door watching them, but they never turned to look at me.

He'll be here. He'll be here if he said he was coming.

My keycard slipped through the lock smoothly. I stepped through the door, wondering: Has everything changed or just me, can everything else be the same and yet so different?

15.
Infinite Samba

MY KEYCARD SLIPPED through the lock smoothly. I stepped through the door, wondering: Has everything changed or just me, can everything else be the same and yet so different?

There was no time for reflection. Tim was already upon me.

"Hi, Daddy. Where've you been? I've been waiting for you. Come, we're playing. In our room. Wait for me there, I'll be right back, I just need to go pee."

Mik called out from the room. I'd imagined his voice would sound as if from another planet when I heard it next, but it didn't. It sounded as though he was calling from my lap.

"Tim? What are you doing?"

"Nothing. Daddy's here."

"Daddy! Daddy! Just in time. Will you help me with this building? It's very complicated. Tim would like to help, but he doesn't know how. He's too small"

"Sure I'll help. That's what I came for."

"Daddy—"

"Yes?"

"You know what?"

"Not yet. I'll know if you tell me."

"*I* don't know how either. I'm also too small."

"Don't worry. Maybe I'm too big. But if we all do our best, we'll manage."

"Great, Daddy. Come quick. We need to do it fast!"

"Take it easy. I need to do a few things first, then I'll join you."

I put the corkscrew in its old place. Let it rest, I won't be drinking wine, and I won't be hacking into the heart of any systems for a while. I put the flowers in a vase and filled it with tap water. I let the water flow over my hands, aware of its beneficial effects. I wanted to cup some in my hands and pour it down my throat but I held back.

Easy. Take it easy. You're not used to it. Mix it with factory-made water. Small amounts at first, then more and more. You need to get used to it. Little by little. Like with water for newborns in Africa. At first boiled water, then some well water added to it, little by little, and after a while only well water. You have to get accustomed to it.

Mik took hold of my hand.

"I'm glad you came home. Now Mommy's left, you know. She'll be away for a while, she said. She says hi."

"Thanks, Mik. Are you hungry? I'm hungry. I'll have something."

"I'm not hungry. We had cookies. And Mommy made vegetable soup for lunch."

Vegetable soup?

"Vegetable soup? Real vegetable soup?"

"Yeah. We helped, you know. We told her it could be instant soup, there are instructions on the package, but she said she wouldn't make instant but the real thing. And we found instructions online and we all helped, Tim cut the tomatoes—"

"Tomatoes? Real tomatoes?"

Mik gave me a surprised look.

"Yeah, real tomatoes. They broke when we squeezed them. A man brought them. He had a beard. He came by bike and whistled. He didn't ring the bell."

Pavel. That was Pavel. Of course, his contact's written down in the pantry. But to think that Monika—

"There's some soup left, Daddy. On the cooker. You can eat it."

I warmed up the soup, bowed my head, shut my eyes, and put the first spoon in my mouth. It was the real thing. It was the taste of the sun and the air. I felt it course through me.

"Did I make good soup, Daddy?"

"You made great soup, Mik. Good on you."

"I didn't make it on my own. Mommy and Tim made it too. We made it together."

"Bravo to all of you."

And to Pavel, for having secretly grown such good tomatoes, and to me, for having written his contact info in such a visible spot that even Monika had found it, and to the sun for shining, and to the air for—

Easy. Easy. Don't get carried away by elation.

With each spoonful in my mouth I felt more at home. When I'd finished the soup, I went into the children's room, and together with the boys we built the buildings from the new Mediterranean kit that comprised the ruins of Barcelona, Dubrovnik, Larnaca, and Haifa, and models of luxury cruise ships traveling between them. The children silently admired our constructions of artful rubble.

I looked in the pantry. There was some food, but I could that see Pavel hadn't brought much. Monika didn't know how to order. I checked our petty cash box. There was some change in there, for a few potatoes and maybe a cucumber.

My account is really empty now. And I'm hungry.

I told the boys to brush their teeth, change into their pajamas, and get into bed. They did everything without protest. When they were already lying down, with their blankets pulled up to their chins, Tim asked:

"What are you going to do now, Daddy?"

"I'll go out for a little while, Tim."

"Uh-huh.—Will you be gone long?"

"No, only a short while. I'll be back before you wake up."

"Uh-huh. Okay."

I placed my hand on the forehead of first one, then the other. Their breathing was peaceful and deep; I could feel sleep overcoming them.

I did not turn on my machines. I took my guitar and tuned it. The first few chords were hard. Then I started to get the hang of it again. I tried to recall some song people would be sure to know, but couldn't think of anything. I considered the national anthem, people were bound to know the anthem, but I wasn't desperate enough for that. I'd think of something to play. I'd start by improvising and maybe something would come to me.

I couldn't find my guitar case, so I wrapped the guitar up in the bag I used for my dress suit. Not wanting to venture far, I went to the passageway outside our local store. Bars and restaurants line the canal further along. When people stopped leaving the store, others would come, headed for food and drink, a lot of people were bound to walk by. Some of them would probably know me. I couldn't decide whether that would be good or bad. I'd see.

I sat down on an empty flower planter and, placing my father's hat in front of me and retuning the guitar one more time, started to play. The underpass added some echo, it was louder than I'd expected. At first the passersby pretended I wasn't there. After a few minutes, the first discount coupon was dropped in my hat. I placed it on the brim and continued playing.

When I returned home, I told myself I wouldn't count the takings until the morning. If this isn't the best of ways to earn some money, I might get some other idea in my sleep. There's no rush. There are still plenty of things I can sell. And maybe Monika hasn't frozen the family accounts. I can check that out tomorrow as well. I'll have to do a simulation: How much we need ourselves, how much we can give to others also in need. I had started too rashly. If I'd disappeared, perhaps no one would've followed in my steps. I'll have to win others over to give this a try.

I listened to the children's peaceful breathing. Then I decided to concede the point: I've come home. I can tear down the wall between me and the world, I won't be inundated.

I played the voice mails. Numerous calls from the Chairman's office, promo jingles, Maya's message that the offer still stood, actually, both offers, more promotional spam. I got to today.

Maya sounded agitated. *No distance? Bad for business, isn't it?*

"Borut, I have something much bigger now. Do you know that I've taken over? The Chairman's vanished. He does an awesome disappearing act, nobody can find where he's gone. South, probably, I know he's transferred most of his assets there, the taxes are lower, in the places where they even have taxes, or it's just cash in hand to the top brass. Anyway, he's gone, adios, bye-bye. And he's appointed me to take over. Drop by some time, we'll do something."

Oh, Maya. You never give up hope. You keep dreaming up increasingly convoluted excuses to satisfy your desires.

I went on to the next message. Monika's voice drifted from the communicator. It sounded as though it hovered, floated, or came from some very large, very faraway land where she knew no one. Quivering. Trembling. A sound of the real world.

"Hi Borut. If you're listening to this, you're home. I hope you've managed your perfect mix. Or whatever."

I have. Perhaps it's not perfect, but it's mine. And yours too, seeing as I've implicated all of you in this.

"Now I'll be gone for a while. Thanks for understanding. One often has to go far away to see things more clearly. Closeness— closeness is pain, Borut. And you know I'm afraid of pain."

I sure do. That's one of the few things I really know about you.

"Thanks for leaving, Borut. It did the trick. I realized that the life we lead is not the only one. Not the only one possible. And I only realized when you were far away that I was far away too, and that I want to be closer to me. Even if it hurts. I realized that as clearly as I finally realize now what I was doing, and as I realize that I'm going to die someday, and that it might hurt. I realize that there's no need to run away from that. Do you know what I'm talking about?"

I do.

"Whatever doesn't conquer love makes it stronger. The weak parts fall off. And then we better feel what we love when we love. Do you understand?"

I sure do, Monika.

"I don't know what you did while you were gone. Maybe I don't even know what you did while you were here. But I do know now that maybe I don't need to know, and I also see that maybe I shouldn't know. You'll tell me when it's over. If you want."

I will.

"Stay if you can. If you can't, let me know. I won't disconnect completely. Until you tell me I can."

She paused.

"I'll be all right. I hope you'll be all right too."

The line goes dead. I wait and wait to hear from you again, but you don't call. There's no rush, though. I have plenty of time. I'm ready. I can wait. And I know I don't have to go looking for you if you're not getting in touch. We'll meet when the time is right. If I stay put for the rest of my life, I know it's not possible that you would never happen by. The kids will grow up. Maybe they'll have kids of their own. Things will move on. I'll do other things right. And other things wrong. And in the meantime, I'll be writing you messages. I know they'll be coming back because the addressee's unknown. But there are things a person must also say, not just think. That's why I have to write you a letter straight away. The first letter. There will be many other letters. Maybe there'll be no end of letters. Things change. Maybe diseases will disappear, maybe we'll never die, maybe our kids won't die either, maybe no one will die ever again. But even if we all die, even if we all die really soon, and even if it hurts, it's important that I send this letter. You hear me, Monika, don't you? You do understand, don't you?

It's time for music again. Not just any music. That immortal Paulinho da Viola piece about watching girls and everything moving on. *Silence, please, while I forget a bit of this pain on my chest. Don't say anything about my flaws.* Then a thousand-beat long break, to see the girls. *Only this love, so laid-back. Whoever knows it all, don't speak. Whoever knows nothing, shut up. If I have to, I repeat it, because today I will make, I will make as I want to, a samba about the infinite.* And not just any version. The one we were listening to the first time we slept together. The one Marisa M sings, the most beautiful woman in the world. You do agree, Monika, don't you? You know I had a picture of her as my communicator wallpaper, not of you; I carried your picture inside me. I was slightly embarrassed about it, it felt a tad childish, so I told you: All you girls with names starting with M are beautiful.

And those with a double M, doubly beautiful. I said that and laughed. But it's true, isn't it? I needn't have laughed. When do emotions become childish and funny? When are we too adult for them? When do you cross the line of not hurting? Whatever is up with you, Marisa? Where have you gone? Did you assume the role of the man from your song, *Profeta Gentileza*, the Prophet of Gentleness, who spent thirty years roaming the streets of Rio homelessly, writing messages of love on walls? I have to go there sometime, to those streets, to read those words. It's not too late, it's not too early, every time is right. After every word there's another, and another, you can never read them all. You've disappeared too, Monika, I could ask what's up with you too, where have you gone. But I won't. I know the feeling. I know you just have to do it when you have to. I did. And I did what I had in mind. And I came back. Nothing has changed. I walked through this door. And everything was as though it were the way it was before. And yet it's all different. Everything changed in an instant.

The door to my room is opening.

"Daddy?"

"Yes, Tim?"

"I was sleeping. Then I woke up."

"I see. Why did you wake up?"

"I was scared you'd left again. You're going to stay now, right?"

"Yes, Tim, I'm staying."

"Yeah. You can leave if you like, you know. But Mik said I should ask. Mik's awake too, you know."

"No, I won't leave. You can tell Mik."

"Now Mommy's left, right?"

"Yeah, Mommy's left, yes."

"What are you going to do now, Daddy?"

"What do you mean?"

"I mean now that Mommy's gone."

"I see. First, I think I'll write something."

"Right.—For work?"

"No, I won't be writing anything for work anymore. I'll write a letter to Mommy. You know something, Tim?"

"What?"

"It's time for bed now. And if you go quickly, we'll fly a kite tomorrow."

"Did you hear that, Mik? Daddy and I are going to fly a kite tomorrow."

"And Mik's coming with us, we're all going to fly kites."

"Right. You're going to fly a kite too, Mik. Daddy?"

"Yes?"

"Aren't we going to preschool tomorrow?"

"No, you're not going to preschool tomorrow because I don't have to go to work."

"Uh-huh. But we're still going to have lunch?"

"Sure we're going to have lunch. I'll cook. Along with the two of you. You're good at cooking."

"Right. But Daddy—"

"Yes?"

"You don't cook as good as the ladies at preschool."

"It's also okay to go to preschool if you'd like, Tim. You can choose."

"OK. I can choose. No. No, I don't want to go to preschool. Is that alright?"

"Sure. Don't worry."

"Daddy?"

"Yes?"

"Are we going to fly a power kite?"

"No, Tim. A regular one, with the wind."

"Right. Because power kites make too much noise?"

"Yes. And because they're not so natural."

"Uh-huh. You know what, Daddy?"

"What?"

"I like the wind kite better. Because you never know where it'll go. You know what, Daddy?"

Tim hugged me, pressing his cheek against mine.

"What, Tim?"

"I have already *figured out* the power kite!"

"Good on you. You're a very bright boy."

"Right. Do you think Mik has figured it out too?"

"I don't know. We'll ask him tomorrow. Now it's time to go to bed, isn't it?"

"Right. Because we're going to fly kites if I go quickly, right?"

"Yeah, go quickly. Maybe Mik's sleeping already."

"Mik's not sleeping. Mik's listening."

"Well, then tell him all about our kite flying and about going quickly to sleep and all that, will you?"

"I will, Daddy. Just one more thing—"

"Tim, if you don't hurry up, we won't have time to go kite flying tomorrow, and I won't be able to write."

"To Mommy? Right. I just wanted to say good night, Daddy!"

"Right. Good night, Tim."

The music fell silent. The children fell silent. Everything fell silent.

Sometimes things must change. And they do.

16.

Let's do it now, let's end this story, you and me, we've waited long enough. You told me to tell you when it's over—it's over now. Everything happens eventually.

Remember the time we flipped through that book with too many colors? Somebody had flown around the world with a camera and viewed everything from the air. You asked me how come I never took pictures, traveling around as much as I did. I like to remember things through my own eyes, I told you. Through my eyes is the right way; my eyes see everything, except me. That's the way I want to remember the world, I told you, as if I hadn't been there. I don't want to be there, I told you, and I said it over and over, and you said I looked just like I was crying.

Well. I didn't want to look like I was crying. Anyway, I didn't want to talk about this. I wanted to say something else: It's here now, this story, all of it. It's here to say: I love you. I know, you're embarrassed, you're thinking this isn't the thing to say, it's too easy. Don't think that. It's not easy.

And don't be embarrassed. It's something you need to know. How many more times in life are you going to hear the words: I love you? They're very important words. You should listen to them.

This story is over. There will be others. There's room in them for you too. And for me. There's plenty of room.

I'm all right. I hope you are too.

About the Author

ANDREJ BLATNIK was born in Ljubljana in 1963. His short story collections *Skinswaps, You Do Understand* and *Law of Desire* are available in English. His books were translated into 14 languages and won some major literary awards in Slovenia and internationally. Blatnik is one of the most respected and internationally relevant post-Yugoslav authors writing today.

About the Translator

TAMARA M. SOBAN is a Ljubljana-based translator. Among other works, she has translated Andrej Blatnik's *Skinswaps, You Do Understand,* and *Law of Desire.*